The Condemned Judge

Studies in Austrian Literature, Culture and Thought

Translation Series

Janko Ferk

The Condemned Judge

Translated and with an Afterword

by

Lowell A. Bangerter

ARIADNE PRESS

Translated from the German *Der verurteilte Kläger*
©1981 Paul Zsolnay Verlag, Wien Hamburg

Library of Congress Cataloging-in-Publication Data

Ferk, Janko, 1958-
    [Verurteilte Kläger. English]
    The condemned judge / Janko Ferk : translated and with an afterword by Lowell A. Bangerter.
        p.   cm. -- (Studies in Austrian literature, culture, and thought. Translation series).
    Translation of: Der verurteilte Kläger.
    ISBN 0-929497-58-9
    I. Title. II. Series: Studies in Austrian literature, culture, and thought. Translation series.
PT2666.E67V4713   1993
838'.914--dc20   92-14029
                                                         CIP

Cover Design:
Art Director: George McGinnis; Designer: Brett Knight

Copyright ©1993
by Ariadne Press
270 Goins Court
Riverside, CA 92507

All rights reserved.
No part of this publication may be reproduced or transmitted
in any form or by any means without formal permission.
Printed in the United States of America.
ISBN: 0-929497-58-9

The Condemned Judge

Justitia has grown old.

The young Justitia abided for centuries, divinely just, meters above the heads of the defendants in the main courtroom. At that time, the judges still wanted to do justice to her. Those days slowly gave way to others.
She grew older.
Today nobody pays enough attention to her. One morning, a lowly bailiff proudly abducted her from the main courtroom and banished her to a musty corner of the cellar, directly below the excrement-stained tract of cells. Cobwebs cover her with silky white nets, and mice run around her. If you really want to—and have the courage—you can still recognize the shadowy outlines of her form, which looks spectrally and hopefully into the past.
Justitia herself no longer takes much pride in her appearance. She is terribly disfigured. Her entire limestone body, which stands on a plinth-

like base, has become chubbier. Her youthful bloom has lost its fragrance. With one hand she holds the weight of a scale that is out of balance; the other rests sadly on her sick heart. Justitia does not see anyone, and tightly around her head lies a disheveled rag that mercilessly covers her eyes; in the old days it was valuable cloth.

She still has all of her body parts. A head that is beginning to seem hydrocephalic and is covered with frazzled hair that looks greasy, disheveled, and unkempt. Her hair is galled. With the passing of time, her nose has become unnaturally discolored. Her ears stand out suspiciously from her head. Her lips are withered, her mouth toothless. Actually, her whole face has collapsed; her forehead has become higher and terribly creased. Her head is still cool. Justitia's lower jaw drops to her breast. She no longer has the necessary strength to close her mouth.

Her neck hardly holds her head separate from her shoulders. Dirty, it juts from the torso.

Justitia's body is covered with fat in every imaginable place. The upper part is made ugly by a terrible sagging bosom whose left nipple protrudes unusually steeply into the air.

Her navel gives the impression of having collapsed, because her belly seems round as a ball and warthoglike and her mons veneris begins lower than usual. Wavy folds that float in the fat *drift quietly around the navel. Her rear end provokes laughter.*

She has the legs of a peasant woman, a working woman, a foolish woman . . . Blocky and watery and covered with varicose veins. She stretches her feet from her body on legs that are knock-kneed.

Not that anybody still takes her seriously. It is not only her ass that is ridiculous.

If she were still alive and not just valuable stone, she would fear being crushed in the rubbish, in which she already experiences difficulty in breathing anyway. Human excrement, which gushes from the defective sewer pipe, already rises far above her ankles.

And in her cellar, Justitia acts like a pedestrian who tries to walk onward without feet.

The theaters play, the brothels are open, the stores sell, and the courts convene. Yes . . . Somebody should pound on the rough table with his bare hand—hard. Then, of course, we would suddenly say no. No . . .

J. Purch lives a life of his own, lonely and alone in his four walls. He is single, without any social life.

When his morning begins like any other, he unwraps himself sleepily and nightmare-plagued from the warm, piled-up bedding. Clothed in linen underpants, he sits down on the edge of his bed, which is covered with white sheets. He slips his feet into the felt slippers that have long since been stretched out of shape, and stares at the bare wall that he faces when lying on his bed. Then he shuffles with sleepy strides into the ice-cold bathroom and bends his naked upper body over the dirty washbasin.

Perplexed, he looks into the scratched mirror. Has he really changed, he asks himself; has he become quieter, or is he suddenly no longer familiar with himself? To be brief, after some marveling, he rejects that annoying question and reaches splashingly for his razor. Slowly the black stubble is separated from the gooseflesh that is suffused with blood. Finally he takes the soap in his hands, evenly lathers his palms, and rubs them over his face, upper body, and carefully but timidly in both armpits. The water sprays eagerly. On the mirror, on the floor, simply in the entire bathroom, water spots form everywhere. Purch rinses off the soap, clumsily catches hold of a hard hand towel, and then stands there dry in nothing flat.

From the bathroom his still wobbly strides lead him to the toilet. He takes down his pants. Urine streams into the toilet bowl. Yellow and lukewarm. Revulsion makes him tremble. He forgets to push the toilet lever and shuffles into his room.

He puts socks on his feet and stretches them tight. After that he fingers a thin undershirt from the chair and pulls it over his head. It lies down coldly against his body. Shivering, he snatches a white shirt from the closet and awkwardly buttons it. As the next step in the dressing ritual he puts on dark blue suit pants; then he puts a narrow cravat around his neck and ties it peculiarly—without a knot; after one more glance into the large room mirror, he goes into the dining room to eat breakfast.

Purch eats cold food in the morning and always prepares his meager breakfast ahead of time the night before. It usually consists of a large apple, a corner of cheese, a piece of bread, and a glass of scalded milk that he salts.

He chokes his morning meal right down. The apple first. Slurpingly, he drinks the salted milk at intervals in the tiniest swallows, or he gurgles it down.

After this meal he leaves everything standing, walks into the outer room, puts on his suit coat, and then dons a tattered interseasonal overcoat besides—*it is autumn.*

Prosecuting Attorney J. Purch stands on the street in front of his home and steers his long strides in the direction of the courthouse in whose lower rooms Justitia found her retirement home.

Simultaneously, from another direction, Miss Lauschig, a young court stenographer, and Judge Peter F. set out for the same destination. Often the two are together all night—without any emotion at all, simply to satisfy their own physical desires. "They exploit each other."

Purch does not think about gratifying himself carnally. The prosecuting attorney occupies himself intellectually. It has always been his dearest wish to become an inventor. That thought has pursued him day and night. But his existence as an inventor has not really been that of a rising star. *He should have left it alone. Should let it be. Not touch it. Not occupy himself with it. A waste of time. Courageously groping his way in foolishness, surrendering himself to something worthless. Abandonment of the intellect to nonsense. Foolish striving toward a goal that has never been properly established. Complete engrossment in an empty cause.*

Purch did not (always) find the right words for himself. While thinking on the way to court, he fell into a jog trot. He drew a lot of attention to his decidedly wretched figure.

The prosecuting attorney limited his world to the daily path from his home to the court and back. (All of that usually at a running pace.)

J. Purch, Peter F., and Miss Lauschig arrive at the court at different times. They reach the court gate panting heavily because they have not been thrifty with their breath. It was the striving of the servants of the court to be overly punctual. They wanted to arrive at the court early, minutes before the beginning of work, and in the evening they voluntarily remained in their stuffy offices past quitting time, without pay, even though the building was repulsive right down to the last detail.

The group of buildings was half-decayed everywhere. The wooden floors, which were pasty with grease, had been gnawed by worms and rats; often the heel of a shoe would strike the damp sand beneath the wooden floor, where mice brought their young into the world. The putrefaction in the cellar had driven the rats to the ground floor.

The judicial establishment appointed too many employees, especially low-level ones, who fled into the rooms in the finished attic, where they quietly slurped their cold malt coffee or café au lait in their work rooms.

And in the attic chambers those people became demented. In those rooms the walls suddenly tipped in front of them. In their absent-mindedness, the bailiffs ran into the walls, banged their heads black and blue, and not only that, but silly as well.

Miss Lauschig was one of the lowest workers. All of the officials who ranked above her (below her were—as has been said—very few!) could scream orders in her face. (One day she would grow deaf because of it, and they would have to give her the rough commands in writing.)

Gradually her associates learned of her relationship with the judge and they gave her a little more respect. Purch, especially, approached her more urbanely day by day.

The well-coordinated trio: J. Purch, Peter F., and Miss Lauschig; the prosecuting attorney, the judge, and the young stenographer spent most of their time together. They were *a single* court unit that instituted legal proceedings, rendered the verdict, and wrote it up in clean copy. It was with good reason that the relationship between judge and stenographer became lively. Purch did not interfere much; if F. was occupying himself with the girl, with complete mental composure Purch threw himself into his work as an inventor. He wrote down data, solved mathematical problems, drew diagrams, rejected the unsatisfactory result, began all over again, and repeatedly toyed with the mistaken notion of completely laying aside this intellectually grueling work.

Peter F. was different. He was pushy. The stenographer offered her entire body to his touch. He nibbled at her opulent breasts, caressed her tenderly behind the left or the right ear. Sometimes he had to scratch her back. She gladly presented her thirsty lips to him for a fleeting kiss.

Purch rejected similar urges and calmly placed himself under the cold shower now and then, from which he sometimes caught colds. After using them once, he threw handkerchiefs away. While he blew his nose forcefully, tears came to his eyes. At night he blew liquid snot into his nightshirt; it seeped through the fabric and penetrated his pores; sweat glands were locally blocked in their activity.

That is how *one* representative of public justice was. His business of state vengeance had become a habit to him—like a love that grows cold as life goes on and is now only exercise. (Exercise: intercourse now and then, which both marriage partners view as unavoidable necessity, or the habitual kiss in the morning before leaving the house for their daily work—both almost a little embarrassed.)

The judge, instructed in the science of law, not only liked to ride his legal paragraphs and handle the sharp and double-edged sword of justice, but also especially liked to find satisfaction for his strong drives. "He often presented the case of his carnal desires before female courts."

He did not owe fidelity to anyone. Not to his law-office relationship; and so far he had not married. So he threw himself with all of his masculine strength into what happened when the urge overcame him. Streetwalkers appreciated him, because he was not ungenerous and also had a respectable prick, as they said.

Other inclinations or curiosities did not trouble him. His work and his favorite occupation absorbed him completely (*and erectly*).

As a judge he always wanted to be just in the investigation and punishment of violence. His sense of justice was very pronounced. Husbands who furiously struck down their wives, crushed them against the wall in their anger, repeatedly broke their bones, beat their bodies until they were sore, and tore almost all the hair from their heads, never received more than half a year in jail. Usually the wives—they were called to the witness stand without exception—tearfully pleaded before the judge for forgiveness for their husbands.

A battered woman who took her miscarried child to its grave, had to do without the presence of her husband at the funeral, because he was still sitting out the prime of his life and his excessive strength (*and freedom*) deep in the dungeon. Both of them wanted *another child*. The man, for fun; the woman, in order not to let her maternal warmth grow cold.

The judge was just—with his truth-loving way of thinking he had spiritually murdered Justitia. His verdicts beheaded her again. "Double decide. Unpunished." Nobody filed an appeal for her. She had nothing with which she could have bribed the lawyers; her great truth was far from being enough for them; she could peddle it to the starvelings of this profession—it would be a waste of time to knock at their doors because none among them ever conducted a major trial, and they would not be equal to this one either, but had already spent their lives squabbling around with the trial of their existence. (In their ground-floor offices, their spirit decayed right next to their papers.)

Late in the afternoon the judge announced to her that her application for a pardon was denied. In spite of that, she learned nothing final;

in the hospital too, of course, you do not learn anything final; nobody says that you will die, although you are already dying. "Death takes you by surprise." *Why should the judge say more than is absolutely necessary and important to "life"?*

"All hope is in vain."

And the judge was not permitted to judge too harshly, nor the prosecuting attorney to prosecute everything. "The world is one single sin." The high court also had to consider the mitigating circumstances: "The side streets in the empty suburb simply invite rape."

By no means could the leniently sentenced culprits know that there were mirrors in the courtroom which showed the judge that they deceitfully tapped their foreheads behind his back. The judge had random thoughts about that.

He also pursued those thoughts. His court liked to convene against new ideas. He did not want to arrest the thinking minds and let their heads roll; rather, he intended to arrest the thoughts in order to protect them from the evil society. Hacking off heads, could that be called *just* judgment? The executioners chopped off the condemned man's head, in which the ideas lay collected, and in that manner satisfied the court's craving. The relatives were permitted to take the body with them and bury it. The head was preserved.

The higher authorities thoroughly enjoyed hearing of such sentences. *With special pleasure.* Many human lives were extinguished to please the high authorities. The judge knew how to fight his way higher step by step. *"He walked over dead bodies."* In his life he had done more asshole creeping than walking erect: that was the reason for his funny posture that fit into few, and therefore only custom-tailored suits. *"How the little children stare!"*

"It is nice when a trial is successful, when justice is tailored precisely to the defendant and it can be said that he died of the death sentence!" he liked to whisper tenderly in the ears of his friends, to whom he had nothing else to say. He did not invent any stories, he was too tightly bound to the truth to do it, and anyway, he thought, he was still too young for that.

The judge was a good person; he did not send his perpetrators to prison, "into that hole!" There they would probably starve and would be punished. He sent them to death—to their final deliverance.

He had the natural talent for bringing fatal order into the wildest life situations of those who were arrested. The prospect of an unending sleep caught many of them by surprise in the very act.

The mothers (and in a few cases the wives) of those who have been sentenced could be called *gushing fountains of tears.*
"DEATH LIBERATES!" he gave the men to take along on the final journey. If there were women in the jail who had to appear before him as guilty parties, he visited them there to converse with them so that he would be able to form a just opinion.
He shoved a glisteningly new banknote into the attendant's belt. The attendants knew what they had to do—they disappeared right then and there.
Then their conversation became more intimate; closer; *cozier.* The young and beautiful women wanted to *give* everything, in order to *survive*—they bashfully gave themselves to him. He avoided the old and ugly ones. There were a lot of attendants who also promised help *to them* and used them to satisfy themselves.
(It even occurred that an older woman prisoner died of a heart attack during sexual intercourse and they later not only discovered her death but also became aware of some threads of semen on her lower body that no longer fit in her sexual organ and made their way into the open. *"She not only gave him her body, she gave him her entire filthy life."*)
While they were still in the prison, distinctions were made: better human goods to the

judge, poorer goods to the lower officials who pressed into the cells with unkind thoughts and full of promises, in order to exploit the women's mortal fear for themselves.

Peter F. could name all the names that were read out at his prisoner's dock. He even liked some of them. Usually he acquitted prisoners who had the same first name as he did. He loved his given name. *Peter.* (Shrewd parents were already beginning to christen their sons with that name as a precaution.)

After the announcement of the sentence he breathed in the vapor of perspiration that had risen from the condemned man while he was in mortal fear of death. He became accustomed to that smell. He already ignored it, just as he overlooked the tears in the eyes of the defendants' mothers.

A judge knew no fellow men. For him there were only the designations: *guilty* and *innocent,* freedom and death.

Peter F. passed judgment only in terms of acquittals or death sentences; a sentence of LIFE IMPRISONMENT seldom crossed his lips.

Justitia threw dark shadows on his body.

The judge took pains with his language. The prosecuting attorney had a supply of empty speeches that he repeated to the point of making his associates impatient. Actually, he only spoke in legal phrases and hardly sought for human terminology. He even intended to use the language of indictments and the court when he composed the patent document for his invention someday.

I am familiar with examples of good citizens. Nobody is turned into a thief and killer by a sense of justice. Devotion to truth can waver no more than a scale for weighing gold. The generated costs of conducting a trial must never become too high. Every complaint must be brought before the judge. People are protected by law. The blows of the attendants' cudgels are childish evidence. The court is just. Arbitrary legal decisions of a few village rulers must be nipped in the bud. Things of an ambiguous nature are made unambiguous by the verdict. The prosecuting attorney has to tear the veil of injustice from the ruling seat of truth. Occasionally judgment may find prison to be warranted. Human oppressors cannot hope for mercy. Obviously, the decrepit official nag must not ride us. Guttersnipes and loafers are wonderful cases for legal action. We must go forward point by point. Not step by step. Unfinished, fragmentary rape is not recognized. Every trial must be conducted. The accused must direct his eyes toward the floor when before the prosecuting attorney. The death sentence that is carried out is no infringement of the right to life.

These character sketches of the judge and the prosecuting attorney reflect their spiritual and moral nature. That is the way they are. And hardly otherwise. "It is seldom that anyone can see into the human being completely."

The judge and the prosecuting attorney.

And the stenographer?

At first she had been a sausage vendor and was studying a little bit on the side in the evenings because she wanted to escape the pawing hands of her lascivious employer. Through a *change of jobs* she intended to change her life. She liked to clasp her hands at her extended back, as she had done in the sausage shop when there were no paying customers.

The ringing of the bell over the entrance to the shop tore her from the worthless daydreams to which she consciously, unconsciously, and zestfully devoted herself—then the proprietor came now and then, nibbling occasionally on a good sausage, blew air that smelled of brandy at her cheeks, and patted her on the right buttock. The rooms of his store were large and extensive. If the present stenographer—still as an evil-smelling offerer of sausage slices—went into one of the rooms and did not find her way out again, the stinking employer was quickly at her side and indulging himself in dubious proposals. He always thought about how he could talk her into an immoral arrangement of the most evil kind—he wanted to do it in all of the deviations from the normal manner, he wanted to try every position, move her up and down on the wall . . . as he had already seen it done somewhere once. Up and down . . . Those were the thoughts that went through his confused mind.

His penis remained erect. Too late he noticed that everything was going into his pants. He had failed again. After such imaginings on his part, he went into the slaughter house, where no work was going on, and assaulted raw chunks of meat that hung down queerly from their iron hooks and sprayed blood. While he made all of this happen, he was very careful to execute complete motions: up and down . . .

At the toilet he aimed wrong and wet the whole floor. The stenographer went to the lavatory *exclusively* at home, because the workplace stall could only be locked from outside and her repulsive employer had already followed her during her first attempt to relieve herself.

She told herself in her overcautiousness that she could not use this closed room that was intended for human necessity.

Among people he was capable of businesslike friendliness and dignified treatment: "Dear Lady! Madam!" If the two of them were alone, he forgot any kind of decency and saw in her nothing more than the object for the *one thing*.

Usually she was afraid she would do something wrong.

Finally he hit her. First with plump sausages, then with his bare hand. Ugly wounds opened on her body. Bowed—and simultaneously somehow proud—she went to court, where she made an accusation against him, and where she met *this* judge. He liked her from the first moment on, at first sight—he immediately propositioned her and promised her a well-paid stenographer position—she accepted. Thus he came *before* and she *to* the court, although she had more likely imagined that she would find a job somewhere unpacking packages. She became tangled in the mesh of this court which drove acquittal into isolation and passed the death sentence even when everything had already been sentenced away and condemned, as in a spider web.

Obviously, the proprietor of the sausage business was subjected to extra special treatment. It was not only that he was charged with several crimes—severe bodily injury, repeated attempted rape, insult, . . . his business was also destroyed and went into bankruptcy. Legal experts resolutely advised him against appealing the sentence of ten years in prison sharpened by a hard bed and once-a-week deprivation of food, because they judged this sentence to be extraordinarily lenient.

In prison he "strolled" in a circle. Round after round.

Finally he only acted the part and hung himself with a lousy bed sheet in his filthy cell.

His eyes bulged from their sockets. He was a horrible sight. He had paid with his life. He was dead. *Physically-spiritually.*

During the first few days the new stenographer did nothing but hesitantly draw letters on sheets of paper. Each letter was thought through three times before it gleamed forth on the smudged slip of paper. Many people wrote difficult foreign words more quickly and less overcautiously.

She squandered her first paycheck on desserts. The judge cleverly took her second one away from her. She believed that she had not so much given it to him as forced it upon him. Slowly she lost her independence and suffered from the fear that she could lose him. A disaster, a calamity, a great misfortune to lose him. "I'll hang myself, really!"

At first she was almost useless in the law office. She was only good for crumpling, for tearing up and throwing away official papers of little importance.

When she felt enough at home in the professional "relationship," she gradually acquired the prevailing contempt for death. A human life that was sentenced to death no longer counted for anything—really, what was it worth?

In her eyes the judge read the desire to be present at an execution, and he fulfilled her wish without hesitation. Hand in hand they attended the event. A lukewarm shiver went down the stenographer's back. "Magnificent!" The judge almost became dizzy, although the condemned man went to his death *like a man*, calmly and *courageously*; he wanted to have nothing at all to do with a priest before his death.

"Those priests! They *can* go jump in the lake!"

For a short time during the execution the stenographer had the feeling that the judge was omnipotent, because he was permitted to decide between life and death on the basis of his own perfect power. He usually decided in favor of the latter.

At that time Peter F. attended the killing of a human being for the first time. He did not like it much. Previously he had never pictured that situation in his mind in detail—now he experienced it, and almost physically. It was an execution by firing squad. A ricochet passed near the judge's head.

Was it intended to be an early warning? It came after the dying man had yet gasped: "You, Judge, you're coming along . . . to Death . . . or he will come and get you . . . yet!" Then there was a pause, and with his last strength the dying man whispered, "Yet . . ."

Then it began to thunder.
Lightning flashed several times diagonally across the sky.
The first rain caught the judge still there.
It had very suddenly grown dark. In the middle of the day.

The stenographer viewed all of this as first-class entertainment and wanted to end that day in a restaurant. Angrily, F. ordered her to go home, where she remained until the next morning, in a bad mood and craving coffee.

From then on the judge was unable to carry on his life freely and without worrying. The freedom that he took from others harassed him. Other feelings sneaked up on him. (His drives remained the same.)

Every day at the same time he remembered the feeling that he had had at the execution. In her humiliation Miss Lauschig did not recognize the problem. She was not capable of understanding his condition. He choked on his feelings, and from that point on he often thought of death.

Peter F. almost envied the prosecuting attorney for his composure. How beautiful everything about his work seemed to him, work that presented him with no misgivings and let him sleep peacefully after cold showers.

Soon F. needed a system for his fears. No condition should get short-changed.

In the evenings and at night he no longer felt tenderness by itself, but rather accompanied by fear of life and doubts of every kind. Because he had lost his self-control to a large extent, his sex life had also grown worse.

Dreams were no longer dreams. They were nightmares.

He was left inwardly divided by the suspicion that Miss Lauschig was responsible for everything and was burdening him down with fears, because it was she, after all, who had had the horrible idea of attending a killing.

They exploited their time together shamelessly. Selfish feelings dominated, feelings that did not close the circle of what they shared in common. They lay in bed, rocking. Independently. They almost forgot that somebody else was there.

The court was never discussed. They did not talk much at all. They remained silent because they had nothing to say. The avaricious judge brought only money matters up for discussion. Nobody wanted to reject the opportunity to meditate. They even economized with light—in his miserliness—electricity was expensive; *"they did it in the dark."*

In the late autumn and winter, in addition to the bad weather, it was also dark when they got up in the morning. In the darkness they separated themselves hesitantly from the nestlike warmth of the bed and quickly endeavored to get on their way to the court. In the mornings all three of them arrived out of breath at the Palace of the Law, as the courthouse was called. In that city, the place of justice was housed in a picturesquely dilapidated mansion on an out-of-the-way street.

The three of them were not the first to be in the *barn* that accommodated the *bureaucratic nag*. Even before their arrival people always turned up in the broad corridors of the court (palace). Without exception they were defendants who were striving for progress in their cases.

The deeds of these people were written on their faces. The judges could just as easily pass judgment based on their appearance. Most of them made little effort to find justice by changing their facial expressions. *"The bureaucratic nag had kicked these miserable criminals in the face after the legal paragraph rider had worked between the horse's thighs."* Their faces were deathly boring; no wonder they wound up with a death sentence.

Such creatures populated the corridors and made rapid progress significantly more difficult. The way was cleared only for the "ladies," whose skirts rustled stimulatingly as they walked. Their painted faces were excited; the corners of their mouths trembled slightly.

It was an experience to hear the sounds of the animated Palace of the Law. Even a fart could be noisy.

Many people hid themselves behind their secret-mongering. They read behind the backs of others or kept their dirty fingernails hidden in their perforated coat pockets.

For bailiffs, even the furnace man, they showed helpless affection. They had the mistaken conviction that he could help them gain acquittal.

They created an obtrusive lack of distance between the court employees and themselves by approaching them too closely. While yet walking away, the lowly bailiffs and the lowest court office workers threw malicious remarks in their hopeful faces. The court had transformed them into unsympathetic beings.

This court was terrifying. The people knew that the officials not only crumbled the bones and shredded the entrails here, they had heard that with their dirty fingers the bailiffs also injured the soul. In any case, that was the worst. They were most afraid of that.

There were people who could move around in complete freedom and often came into the courthouse to experience something. They wanted to feel the fears of the condemned, smell their sweat, inhale the breath of death.

They expected something special, looked forward to any event—and nevertheless took each and everything as it came.

In general there was no trust; they distrusted rather than trusted. Trust did not arise, neither between the fat ones nor among the thin ones; *nobody trusted anybody*, least of all themselves; everybody was afraid of failing miserably beneath the hail of questions from the judge or the prosecuting attorney. The court's victory was assured.

"The bureaucratic nag produced so much manure that individuals had to surrender themselves completely to their queasiness." If they did not feel well and could not spit, they stuck one finger deep into the throat and vomited where they were standing. The vomit sprayed widely in the vicinity and stank clear into the last nook and cranny of the mansion.

The judges and prosecuting attorneys, and only they, experienced feelings of victory. Once and for all, they had defeated everyone whom they had driven to death. *"The nag had neighed at them for the last time."*

They delighted in the fact that their existence as victors was based on the situation of defeat. *Their victory was simultaneously a defeat. Like in the war. Winners and losers. And war is no game. Not a style of play for childish generals. "Heroes die there!"*

There were people who treated themselves to their meager breakfast—the only meal of the day—in those rooms. Their palates twitched imperceptibly. Their saliva lost itself in the mush. Their teeth chopped everything to the same size. Their stomachs made no distinctions. They became sated. They simply needed the right amount.

Now and then rough brawls occurred. Slowly one blow after another fell. They were in the courthouse, and the way it went was: An eye for an eye! A tooth for a tooth! "That extremely ordinary mode of retaliation."

Sometimes a set of false teeth with undigested breakfast fragments in the spaces between the teeth fell heavily to the floor; quickly enough somebody destructively placed a foot upon it. A glass eye with a squeezed out tear did not remain whole for very long.

Lavatory lights carved busily flashing eyes in the thick air.

In the men's rest room they once found the unmoving, stinking, and battered corpse of a woman. Attendants rapidly carried her to the cemetery on a broken bier and buried her without coffin or flowers. Nobody reported the dead woman missing. *"She died impersonally."* Another time a man's body in the women's lavatory frightened the "ladies."

Everything had been brought into disarray, sent into hopelessness, driven into degeneracy.

From time to time one could gape at certain women in the building corridors. *"Whores in the palace."* There they warmed themselves and hoped that someone would put them in a cell by mistake—it would be a nice shelter for them.

Their desire, if they still felt any, was painful; it curdled their blood. They had long since been giving themselves for nothing. In their run-down condition they no longer found paying customers. Their bodies were emaciated and their pubic mounds probably looked gaunt. Men whose penises went into their lower bodies had to have fallen very low.

Their main thought was to stop living.

The feeling of guilt at not having accomplished anything in life got the upper hand; it was suicidal.

They were still able to make decisions but gladly rejected the achievements decided upon.

During their stay in the building they were apathetic and lost themselves in the crowd of court visitors. In the lavatory they sighed and leaned their weary heads against the shit-covered wooden wainscotting that was disfigured with indecent, shameless, and offensive pictures and characters. *"Where people put their abominations."*

In order to justify their presence there, to which they were implicitly obligated when at the courthouse, they tried to press excrement out of their behinds, in vain; nothing fell into the toilet bowl. They wadded up paper, and to the neighboring stalls they dedicated the noises that should likewise justify them. Carefully, they opened the door latch. Someone already stood outside in front of the door, somebody who was trying to vomit.

Windows slammed shut in the draft, which tore them out of their daydreams.

In the waiting rooms the impatient people addressed passing court workers by the names that they had already learned long ago. In order to draw attention to themselves, speaking people went hopping after those who were addressed. With the grace of fools, they looked into their eyes; they seldom received an answer—the result was offended shrieking, bawling, gnashing of teeth, screaming, . . . sometimes weeping without tears. But: Men's tears also flowed, and when they did, there were actually torrents of men's tears. *"I haven't cried for a long time. Today it's as though my whole body were thawing and pouring itself out in ridiculous tears."*

These people were already disappointed before the first light of day and could not recover from it all day long. Faces that they pulled while filled with anger even made them far more morose.

Objects were not placed on display; a thief would have soon turned up who would have *securely* stowed the things elsewhere.

There were no flowers, nobody had a feeling for them. The high rooms were undecorated.

Those who wanted to read could read "SPITTING PROHIBITED," and for revenge they resisted that order. Others imitated them in order not to fall out of the picture or out of character. The judges slipped and almost fell on the slippery floor, and after every occurrence of that kind, they lashed out wildly. *"This attack is called self-defense."*

Nobody washed the windows that had gone blind; you could see neither out nor in. The place was never aired out, it was stifling.

The jaws of many court visitors dropped; saliva flowed from their mouths. Bailiffs hit them hard there in passing—with the key ring that each of them carried in his hand. It was not absolutely necessary that the key was given or had been given a task, it was simply a status symbol.

If someone was hit, he flew at the bailiff with his bare hand—half numb with pain—and stomped on his foot. In saying "Ouch!" they behaved like animal tamers or knelt down, rubbed their shoes, jumped up, and turned cartwheels. When they did that, blood rushed to their faces. Most evident in spite of everything were their buffoonish noses.

The attendants were abusive by agreement with the higher authorities and were never taken to task. Halting narratives given before the examining magistrate by people who had been thrashed to the ground were silently passed over.

These people only knew caresses for their "peers."

Their situation was difficult, dangerous, and uncomfortable. For that reason they also found nobody who pulled them out.

They no longer wore a (black) suit, but now only a ragged loincloth that they ashamedly wrapped around their hips. *"Muscle atrophy comes from not working, and a fat belly from eating too much."*

They waited away their lives in the courthouse. *"They took the little children along to wait. They became completely apathetic."* Calmly the judge sent them to death on the basis of the evidence. This man determined their destiny, especially their mortal destiny.

In spite of everything, patience was their strength. If they were called before the judge after a long time, in order to defend themselves personally in their case, they became overzealous in their thanks and joy: *"Everything is mercy."* The official who passed judgment threw them out of the room, unvictorious and with nothing accomplished. They began waiting again. *"In the meantime the little children had already become bored."*

Blind people who came into the courthouse and said: "I can see nothing," were told: "There is nothing to see!"

There were doorknobs only inside the room. Defendants could not open the doors when they wanted. They were *admitted.* Clerks were accustomed to using the secret (mystery) doors or the outside doorknobs that they carried with them in their pockets.

(The prosecuting attorney met this intrusion like a grandmother. He entrenched himself behind blindness, deafness, and muteness. Thus he arrived in his office almost undisturbed. Of course he had to shove some bodies out of the way in order to hold office in state service, *"in order to ride the bureaucratic nag."*

Every morning, Peter F. hoped once again to be the first person in the office. He therefore always tried to unlock the door. The key could not be turned. The door was unlocked. That was the most certain sign that the prosecuting attorney was already present.

A repulsive liquid ran out of the judge's mouth. Foaming at the mouth with anger, he reproached himself for not having been there earlier. Desperately, he held the key in his hand and did not want to drop it into the inner pocket of his coat.

After the judge, the stenographer arrived in her place—very pale, she appeared (to the people) almost chalk white. She smiled as though she had some adventure in mind. She was wrapped in warm clothing. Her lips had lipstick on them, her eyes glittered impudently.

The judge often asked himself what would have happened if she had not burst into his life.

From her he had learned that women have a different kind of common sense and different mores than men, and that for the most part they form no preconceptions *"Ideas about the low worth of life."* Perhaps she was an exception.

Miss Lauschig said nothing disadvantageous about herself. After all, people are not forced to claim bad things about themselves. *"I have a good opinion of myself and about myself and for myself and against myself."*

She was not a girl with strict principles. Meanwhile, the judge directed her work anyway.

With the indication that she did not know the consequences, she rejected many things. (Never an orator, she was always an accuser.) She did not yet worry about spending her old age free of worry. *She* did not propose marriage to Peter F., she was afraid he could turn her down (as they say), and besides that, she did not yet think that she had framed such a proposal in words that satisfied her.

Miss Lauschig did not dare become recalcitrant toward Peter F. in any way. He was the most influential man that she knew. In the meantime, she had already settled accounts with the highest and final judge.

Her tendencies were extremely comical. With respect to the administration of justice she had the peculiar (amazing) notion, to which she could not give utterance, that the justice should still be discovered, that condemned everyone except the prosecutors.

Besides that, she had the idea that the sense of justice must affect everyone, and that one must force it upon the person to whom it was foreign, for the world is wicked and somebody must constantly be penalized and punished. (She found a degree of satisfaction in her profession.)

If she arrived at a dead end with her argumentation—in conversations with the prosecuting attorney and the judge—in order to be able to leave the room, she fled into a coughing spell that did not seem to quit. When she returned to the office again, after half an hour had passed, the conversation had long ago since been forgotten, and a fuss was being made about other things.

When she spoke of liberation, she cursed and blasphemed, although in doing so she only wanted to hide the defiance that she had still retained from the time of her puberty's onset.

At the court she had achieved a certain rank—the judge had been of assistance to her. Out there in the world she was the nameless woman; that hurt her; that injured her; that cut her to the quick. It was revolting to her to be a mass consumer of mass-produced goods when she went shopping. The thought of being a stranger among strangers in the theater ignited within her a fire that blazed with masses of flames—she wanted to be Miss Lauschig, the stenographer, the person she was, only that, not simply a person or a number like the people to whom the court denied forever the right to life. As the wife of a judge she would be something after all, not simply the little girl whom nobody knows and nobody wants to know. "The judge's wife!"

On a morning like any other, the prosecuting attorney, the judge, and Miss Lauschig remembered that they had another case to pass sentence on. The hearing had already taken place, the judge had made his announcement, the written verdict would follow—now they were engaged in putting it on paper. This act of putting the verdict on paper was something that they knew by heart, something that they reeled off quickly in the usual manner.

Peter F. recited his decision to Miss Lauschig slowly, because she wrote at the same rate. The prosecuting attorney listened. Now and then he gave voice to his concerns, upon which long discussions followed, which the stenographer ended by interrupting the debate with stupid questions. Then they let her decide who would finally be right in the end.

Actually, one should ask the question: How does the transcription or record of such a verdict read?

"In the primary hearing on such-and-such a date, the accused, A., was found guilty. He has to answer for his actions.

"During the hearing, A. proved to be eager to talk, and in addition to his speeches that did not seem inclined to end, he was to be envied for the deep sadness that caused the time to pass more easily for him and showed him to the court as good, strange, sad, and unapproachable.

"Beside himself with limitless admission of guilt, he tried to carry out an awkward dance before the eyes of the illustrious prosecuting attorney, the frightening judge, and the honorable court stenographer. His music was the thumping and banging of those who were waiting in front of the main courtroom. Then the sun came up slowly—we began the hearing early—and tickled his open eyes. A ray struck his comical expression, the description of which is not necessary here.

"In response to the prosecuting attorney's strong objections, the accused was ordered to stop. In this connection a senior attendant distinguished himself, stopping him with a hard, albeit not rough grip.

"I asked him who he was, where he came from, and where he might want to go.

"Reflecting for a long time, he closed his eyes; later he suddenly shouted the answers with emphasis into the quiet of the room.

"He said he was the accused A., a man with few needs, who no longer had any personal memories, except one, specifically the one that reminded him of his last classes in school. To be sure, he had had some thoughts about his origins, he said, but he had soon forgotten them. He had tried to remember, but he had not yet been able to think—until now—because, of course, he had *had to* dance and then had been roughly handled.

"To the impertinent and tactless, yes, even curious question of where he came from, he could give an only partially satisfactory answer, he avowed.

"He had come freely from life and had traveled through the world, until one day, without even quietly questioning him in advance, they had arrested him. This detention had crippled his subconscious inner involvements, he claimed, and he demanded compensation in money, he stated.

"Beyond that, between his remarks about his origins, he described the stenographer as totally whimsical and inwardly at odds with herself.

"Because of this compulsion to speak, without transition he suddenly talked about something harmless. He concerned himself with the immortality of the soul and supposedly wanted to emphasize the senselessness of a death sentence—in any case, that is what the prosecuting attorney claimed to have understood his thoughts to mean.

"Intermittently he asked about the progress of the prosecutor's invention. He drew attention to the fact that they had known each other for a long time, and simply to be courteous he had to ask about its progress. On the other hand, they met infrequently and he had no other choice but to misuse the main hearing to ask about his activity as an inventor. He suggested advertising the invention on large billboards in the streets of the suburbs. The prosecuting attorney should write the material about the invention in a foreign or even dead language, in order not to neglect or disadvantage the rest of the world with respect to its existence.

"A. himself felt more than ever that he had been treated meanly because he had blond hair and blue eyes.

"By and large the answer was not very clear and was like a rumor on a small-town side street.

"He visibly shrank back from answering the third question. He preferred to embark on silent observations of nature and in so doing effected a waning of his sense of reality. The earlier condition, which obtained prior to his answering the first question, could not be restored. The prosecuting attorney once more voiced objections about that, to which A. quietly responded that he could not disturb him in that manner, but only entertain him.

"Without possessing the proper authority, Prosecutor Purch permitted him to stand comfortably because he was, after all, a human being.

"Finally he hinted that he would answer the third and last question, the inquiry concerning his possible demise.

"The high court, as he said, knew that he was a thinking individual with some creative imagination, whose personal feeling of solidarity would never permit half an ego to make itself independent in order to take a different direction than the first half of the ego. This danger always existed, he believed, because general consumption cracked open not only the character but also the personality. In spite of everything, the court would never succeed in finding the thinking self separate from the creative self. He would see to that, he threatened—with a raised index finger.

"Without great speeches, we must recognize that it is our task to explain clearly to the accused whether his deed inclines more toward acquittal or toward a death sentence.

"First we point out to the accused the elements that speak in favor of acquittal.

"Actually, acquittal is not profitable for anyone.

"It is completely according to the old school to acquit the condemned; acquittal only sets criminals in motion, into free life, and starts them toward new deeds. They are only the curly-haired wind-up dolls of possible crimes.

"The court should direct acquittal toward isolation. Acquittal should end in sad loneliness. With acquittal, one pampers both the guilty and the innocent perpetrator. In any case, the death penalty is nothing bad. The acquitted person barks at the court personnel anyway.

"The acquittals that have been pronounced to date contain the price that we must now pay for general freedom: We share freedom with criminals, rapists, slanderers, cat-killers, and sometimes even with murderers.

"Life is in constant competition with death—and the court has the responsible duty to combat this active discord.

"The supply of death sentences is large, of course, but the demand is small. In spite of that, we somehow get along. Occasionally we must feel the death of a condemned person; that lies in the hands of the judge. The feeling cannot be pretended, it must be experienced. The prison cemetery must not be a failure in planning and must become too small.

"People look into the deathly earnest eyes of these sentences, without appreciable concern, because they still do not comprehend their great meaning. 'If at least the side glances were appreciative.'

"Does nobody fear for his well-kept, delicate body parts? After all, a criminal could—in his insane fury—seriously injure somebody there. Does nobody really think about what his future would be like then?

"Those people will be recognized by their movements, as the lame are by theirs.

"The defendant A. must, in any case, be condemned justly. It was he who spit in an attendant's face, after the latter called him a pig.

"Every defendant is tastelessly ordinary, shapeless, and unmusical. If he was not that way before, then he acquired these traits during his detention prior to trial—and such people have played out their right to life. We could carry their ashes in a dustpan and dump them on a garbage heap; it would be a waste of a beautiful place in the cemetery.

"After the *death* sentence is passed, the rest of their life should be so short that they can no longer count to ten—in that time.

"(If they live longer, they only remember their sensitive sexuality anyway, that was deadened from moment to moment by the beauty of gratification. After intercourse, such a man's penis was numb, without feeling, ugly, deformed, smaller, and not an exact concept.)

"It has been proven that next to the defendants' eating, and perhaps the passing of time as well, thinking about women and intercourse is the primary activity of the condemned.

"During the pronouncement of sentence, they experience the uniquely monumental feeling of no longer being permitted to live. Powerfully. They were strong if they steadfastly transformed their weakness into strength and overcame the fear of death, which does not exist anyway, rather, only fear In the face of death. But they probably never recognize that.

"The pronouncement of the death sentence should simply be canceled, and the criminals should die in uncertainty. Our arrangements pertaining to death are much too good.

"That is how the matter of acquittal looks; we still have the task of explaining the death sentence and its advantages.

"After the pronouncement of the death sentence, feelings are experienced more consciously. The condemned hear time knocking, their hearts beating. They look at themselves and recognize things *about their actions.* If they look even deeper, they recognize *causal* things. They fear loneliness. Then they feel death so strongly that their hearts almost stop. They find themselves in a time that is empty of human beings. For them, all that counts is the private disgusting self. Then they do not waste another moment, and they reproach themselves horribly: Why did we not live our earlier lives this way?

"They praise their past because they have no future, although only the past has caused their future to be canceled.

"They want to tell everyone something more, the judge, who comes again, about their first toy; and to the priest they confess their first experiences with a woman. Many have something more to say about their dear mothers.

"They no longer want to exhale, because it could be the last time.

"*Out and in. Back and forth. Here and there. Hither and yon. Now and then. Strike and strike back.*

". . . Suddenly they speak hastily and in memorized phrases; nothing more must go wrong. They say a word and you already know what they want to say, because you know the expression. They no longer speak, they shout in order not to be ignored.

"While their final breaths still last, they no longer look anyone in the eye. There is nothing new to see in the eyes of strangers anyway.

"With their deaths everything that they once were is destroyed, even their outrageous deeds. For those reasons, the death sentence.

"Following these comprehensive explanations, back to A. In the meaningless hearings he confessed that he had lied to people, wanted to kill his teacher, stolen things at the weekly market, injured the feelings of the world, nibbled at unwashed earlobes, swum naked at dawn, been unfriendly, talked to himself, removed chunks of mud from his shoes, failed to confess mortal sins because the priest constantly interrupted him with stupid comments during his lip service.

"That is already too many offenses for a death sentence. What can you do? Everybody knows that our administration of justice is lame. We should immediately call a state of emergency and place the responsible parties before us judges.

"Time is passing. The court must deprive A. of his last hopes, especially his zest for life. He must recognize that he will lack nothing, when he is *then finally* dead.

"But his inclination to speak in front of the judge must not degenerate into speechlessness before the highest judge.

"A. can be permitted to retain his capacity for sympathy, he can be allowed to mourn for himself.

"I pronounce the sentence:

"The accused, A., is sentenced to death and will soon no longer be permitted to live. He may select the manner of execution for himself. If his inventiveness is limited, he will die by hanging. If, contrary to all expectation, he should survive this divestiture of life, he will be regarded as a new person."

With these words F. closed the condemnation of the defendant A. In so doing, he began sweating so much that he had to wash his hands and use a towel. Actually, he should also have changed his shirt.

Lost in thought, he scratched his butt and encouraged the embarrassed, long, and awkward silence of Purch and the stenographer, who brushed mouse droppings from the top of the desk with her left hand, just as though she were poking around in a wasp's nest. The judge wanted to give further directions for polishing the document, but he was not a person who interrupted an ongoing standstill agreement. Finally, however, he could no longer hold back after all.

"Once more I have closed up the asshole of an enemy of the social order!" Peter F. said and was satisfied with himself. "He will not take advantage of us any longer."

In the eyes of the defendants, Peter F. was a rotten rat; he knew neither honor nor shame. "I'll spit into the mouth of that body yet!" an arrested man promised. After he had done that he was beaten until he acknowledged that he had not and had never been beaten.

They seemed to have run out of things to talk about. In order to lead them out of the painful situation, the stenographer spoke of the judge's death-bed and expressed the hope that it would not be her bed. The judge's ears actually pressed back against his head in panic.

"Miss Lauschig!" he began. "You don't know what you're talking about. That's not like you. Usually you are more reasonable! Do I perhaps already have the face of a dying old woman? Dying's centrifugal force does not move me yet. I do not yet dream of dying. Before *I* die, the saliva in *your* mouth will turn sour! Besides, I like to go to the theater," he said, slammed his glass down, left the law office early—in contrast to his usual practice—and went home ahead of Miss Lauschig, where he waited for the arrival of her sex organ, in order to sate his *feelings* with it. Her head caused *him* to ache. His caress tickled her. She put her hand on his shoulder.

Far away, the barking of mongrels resounded. All at once he felt sick as a dog. Time had passed. The death bell rang briefly. He had to finish remembering. In his agitation he could not prevent mental leaps.

A pause breathed loudly and gave birth to silence. His body was warm, his heartbeat almost normal again.

A final way out. A final excuse—not a contradiction, just a nasty feeling. He was already itching again—a good sign. He would throw himself on the stenographer's body again and place her on the floor of accomplished facts. He took her from behind and did it in the manner that he carried out the routine of his appointment book: without feeling, planned out, and almost with an animal eagerness to work.

Peter F. felt heavy, awkward, and sore.

The next day he was supposed to go to work again. *"The legal-paragraph rider would not neglect to throw oats to the official nag for its feed."*

In his free time the prosecuting attorney was totally different from the judge and the stenographer. He was nothing but an inventor. The condition of being entirely an inventor suited him tremendously. He addressed his work almost without feeling.

Purch was firmly convinced that someday his work would be a worldwide success, if it only came out in the form of a patent. Contrary to the opinion of the accused and henceforth condemned A., the presentation of the prototype would not be in a foreign language. To his inventive way of thinking, he did not want it to be esoteric, but modernly and professionally clear.

To be sure, he intended to do away with everyday loquaciousness and cheap humor, even in the rough outlines.

Purch asked himself half aloud and seriously: "When will my time come?" Somebody said to him: "Your time will come later!" It was no pure pleasure to be an inventor. Beyond that, within his four walls he behaved introspectively, as if playing things to the end, transcendentally, and in accordance with a Christian interpretation of history. His movements were not precisely calculated or planned. Nevertheless, they had their meaning, and none arose out of chance. Why, he could not say.

In his home Purch was monstrous and demanded to be the center of attention. In his farcical state of wakefulness he played out nightmare scenes that were sometimes sensitively and melodramatically, sometimes degradingly and cruelly left to their own devices. The sentimentality longed for cruelty, and the cruelty dragged itself into the sentimentality. But raw violence was always more or less an older friend that appropriately moved things along from one to another. His sparse clothing played the most important supporting role.

"Am I obliged to release even the first impression? Can I refuse to give my invention over to worn-out colloquial language?"

If he reflected for a long time, he developed a headache that permitted the dreamy journey to come to an end or directly forced it to do so. For obvious reasons, he then cursed his head and felt painfully touched by illness throughout his body. Purch endured his body.

His mornings, his evenings, and his nights unrolled as if in forced repetition; nothing new happened; for that reason he also made no progress—in his laborious work. Every night he enthralled and dazzled himself anew, although he only moved on in the process of aging.

Late at night he went to bed and in the mornings he felt like he had slept in a ditch, because his whole body was as though it had been beaten sore. Suddenly he exchanged the concept "bed" for the word "ditch" and said "ditch" instead of "bed" and "bed" instead of "ditch."

In the dream (of his sleep) he was always being beaten—to a little pile of bones, flesh, blood, shit, and urine. When he awoke, it was for him a relief and a release.

"If a morning begins for him like any other, he unwraps himself sleepily and nightmare-plagued from the warm . . . bedding. Clothed . . ."

Purch was supposed to go to work.

At work he encountered the judge and Miss Lauschig who had spent a difficult night.

Miss Lauschig was shattered. Peter F. had jumped around on her like on a young creature. She remonstrated constantly that she had been treated negligently. During their deliberations, she did not have to suppress laughter, because the matter was serious to her. Peter F. went too far, she thought, when he demanded it three times—received it as a gift twice, and the third time obtained it almost by force. Hell could not be worse.

After quitting time, she voluntarily walked home. Miss Lauschig threw endearments in Peter F.'s face, perhaps from force of habit or to pass the time.

In the neighborhood her reputation fell on bad ground, she was considered to be immoral, sinful, somewhat dubious, and whorelike. Many claimed that she was a danger for the children.

The judge was a zealous theatergoer.

Now and then they woke up together during the night. *At night there were constantly surprises. Time never stood still then (unfortunately).* "That is no reason to worry."

In their wakefulness the two of them listened to the street. *Nothing happened. Nobody came; nobody went. It was terrible.*

Occasionally their arms then wrapped around each other's bodies and they fell asleep, cramped together.

Often they closed their eyes, turned over on the other side, and fell asleep. Without being angry, they woke up in the morning and had to go to work.

On Sundays J. Purch remained in bed for a long time. With the help of a hand to shade them, he protected his eyes from rays of the sun that came in. Thrown from the peaceful and satisfied embrace of sleep, every Sunday Purch considered anew what he should do. He wanted to sleep until noon, then dine in the best possible manner, and after that still take a short hike. After an hour at most, he wanted to go home.

Instantly he gave himself to his work. He always forgot again where he had left off and started over from the beginning; for that reason there was no progress in the project.

In innumerable conversations with himself J. Purch said, "It is not enough to have lived, one must also have worked."

The seasons were all the same to him. *"He always heard the quietness of the landscape re-*

main silent": in the falling of the winter snow and in the thunder of the summer storm. He only tolerated the generally accepted truth that in the winter night falls much earlier, and he turned on the light earlier in order to avoid the "dangerous darkness," as he called it.

(His profession was to shine light into difficult cases by bringing them before the court and requesting the judge to pass sentence.)

On Sundays Purch was at home almost all day.

Peter F. and Miss Lauschig did not resemble him in the least in their Sunday time arrangement. (They were younger, more gluttonous, and above all less experienced.)

They sometimes argued about their routine for the day. One word led to another, and the loudest argument had broken loose. One tried to outyell the other. Miss Lauschig closed her eyes while yelling, in order to give herself over completely to arguing. So they clamored away a part of the day with useless yelling that only brought confusion where there had been order. The quarrel was clearly reflected in the feelings of the two of them: They were ill-humored and moody. Harsh epithets fell. And they were constantly looking for other names. In fun it would be amusing to argue. The two of them scolded themselves hoarse and only fell silent when the voice of one gave out. Then the one who could still croak a little bit was tenderly concerned about the other, and the worst epithets had vanished like smoke. *("Little misery. Stuck-up laying hen. Spoiled licking female. Horrible judgment pronouncer. Repulsive paper crumpler. Asshole.")*

As stated, the Sundays that were spent in name-calling were an exception. Usually this free day passed more peacefully, perhaps more pleasantly.

They slept longer and had intercourse once more. Although they had enough time, they made love hurriedly, as if in a fever, like sick people. (She uncovered her breast with wistful charm.) It was nice to sleep long. A boon, after they had had to get out of bed very early all week long. On Sundays they simply wanted to sleep a long time. Nor did they awaken each other—from their sleep.

If one of them was awake, he got up and did not disturb the other's state of rest and inactivity. But the difference in their times of awakening was usually only half an hour, so the one who woke up first was lonely for only half an hour. He turned plans over in his mind about what he could do. There was only one thing that he did not want: to wake up the other person. That would be a serious breach of agreement and cause for an argument in one. (A splendid case for these myrmidons.)

When both were awake, Sunday finally began. Sunday! What is there still to describe at length and in detail? Undertakings that arose out of the current situation? Toward evening a cup of strong coffee and a piece of sweet pastry, then pause ( ) until evening and the walk home closely arm in arm.

Sometimes in the evening they also attended a boisterous dance, although the two would rather be alone, undisturbed and secure in their reciprocal embraces. Besides that, he was a rather poor dancer. He preferred to go to the theater.

They stood in the middle of life. They believed that they stood well. Together they stood on four feet.

Not everyone gave themselves up to this untouched affectedness and beauty. People whom the court drew into its grip unwillingly slapped themselves with their own thoughts concerning the court, the administrators of justice, and the entire legal system. "The rock on which the court was built is called fear."

Many thoughts were deep and mature, they would have taken effect if they had not come from the evil-smelling mouths of defendants who were destitute and ill from drinking booze. But there were also sober people who did not spit a good word at the court. "Its knives are sharp."

There was much to complain about. Those who objected went from point to point and embarked upon wild reviling that would have encouraged the lowest bailiff—if he had heard something—toward a flowering defamation-of-character suit. *"The official nag is a paralyzing old mare, and the legal-paragraph rider is an impotent nudist who is completely exposed by any law, no matter how wretched."*

Yes, . . . No, . . . Perhaps, . . . Perhaps, it may be that they were not incorrect in their assumption. In any case, severe accusations were voiced against the court summoners, bailiffs, and executioners, as well as their innumerable subordinates. *"The death-blow will strike the official nag, the first stream of blood will drown the legal-paragraph rider . . ."* You heard: The lawyers create nothing but conflict and hate. Hate and conflict. And jealousy. They divide humanity into two large camps, into the ragged tent of the defendants and the lofty mansion of the prosecutors. The lawyers reduce people to offenders. They impose guilt upon them.

And the court first: The court creates and causes crime. Without the court there would be no deed, the court fathers it first.

And further: It is really the case, one can condemn the court, it is not a lie, they are simply telling the great truth. There would be evidence.

As long as he does not come in contact with the court, the individual has incorrect ideas about the administration of justice. If realization begins, it is usually fatal. The defendant hardly has enough time left to think about how young he is.

Again and again you hear of shameless and shocking, even sexually deviant encroachments by the judges.

Some time ago, such a (middle-aged) judge crept into a public garden. *"Like a culprit."* In that fact alone there would still be nothing abnormal, but the judge was thinly clothed. He wore only an old hat whose leather gleamed black with grease, a shabby coat, thick woolen stockings, and worn-out boots.

The hat fit poorly, the socks slowly slipped deeper, the bootlaces were untied, and the buttons of the coat were not in the buttonholes. The lawyer's hands were stuck loosely in the coat pockets, but firmly enough to cover the jurist's nakedness. Under the coat he was just as the creator had placed him into his creation, the world.

It was already late, but in the garden it was still light to some extent.

The judge strolled like a thief through the public garden. At first he walked like a criminal.

And then like a traitor who could be bought. He looked around suspiciously.

When everybody had left the garden and only a young woman remained in the park, his time had suddenly come. He strutted onward. *"His balls rocked loosely in the evening twilight."*

His body trembled—not because of the cold, it was warm enough, but for the sake of the longed-for deed toward which he hotly and feverishly moved. He could hardly wait for "his moment." With the wet tip of his tongue, he traced around lips that felt like bursting from the skin; his nose trembled when he breathed, his eyes bulged lasciviously from their sockets, and sweat flowed across his forehead.

The woman came slowly toward him with measured strides. (The judge did likewise.) The distance between them diminished step by step. They had approached each other.

At the moment when she looked into his sick eyes, she suddenly became unspeakably afraid . . . then he quickly (as quickly as possible) tore open his coat and showed her *his sex organ between his legs.*

The woman strangled her screaming and ran (as though in shock) away. She would not be able to forget that sight for a long time, not because of the naked penis, no, she was familiar with such a thing already, of course—not only from hearsay. He had smeared his lower body with an animal's excrement and he gave off a terrible stench. And from the animal excreta projected a hard piece of flesh that she would never ever let penetrate her belly. This encounter brought her an experience that led to her constant anxiety from then on. After that she was no longer responsive in the normal way in that respect. Listlessness spread through her body, a new feeling that she had never known before.

The judge was certain of that; he grinned devilishly and marched home—satisfied and at the same time somewhat aroused. During the walk home he masturbated onto the street. The semen that he flung to the ground became soiled with dust.

The next time he intended to visit another garden and smear the excrement of a different animal on his abdomen. For variety he could then still anoint his body with his own.

Before the court Peter F. interpreted the law literally and based himself—with hands and feet—entirely upon the laws. He was completely covered by the law, which he often stutteringly read aloud. Other judges spelled out emergency powers acts in this disgraceful manner. It was a poor (wretched) situation. The jurists themselves were already beginning to speak of the state of legal emergency. Not only the act of uneducated reading was devastating, but mice also gnawed on the documents, on the chairs, simply on the whole system.

Peter F. supposedly passed judgment unprejudicially. That he did not like one nose or some clothing or other, meant nothing; that was no prejudice, it was a personal disinclination toward this and that.

The bailiffs had long since made that discovery about F.'s personality in order to have something to talk about while they waited for assignments in their small offices. They were not permitted to show themselves in the courthouse corridors without work, because their clothing was scanty and not in keeping with their rank. The court, however, could not purchase any new clothing, because the judges constantly demanded higher salaries and received them, of course, because if they did not, they refused to pronounce death sentences any longer.

The death sentence was the crowning achievement in the administration of justice. The courts fought for the honor of the higher ratio of death sentences. *"Only the pronounced death sentence makes the young judge a judge who passes judgment correctly!"*

Shortly before dying, the dull faces of those who were sentenced to death were sketched in black and white. The sketches were placed in the records of the judgments that resulted in death.

Quickly, they still silently or moderately loudly recited a prayer, or spoke one with a sharp voice, which, next to the burning candle, kindled a mood that was shrouded in mystery.

Some of those who were destined to die still emptied a glass that had been filled with cheap liquor, others drank juice, some of them coffee, a few water. In despair one of them once even ate his own shit.

"They saw death. With that their vacant gazes broke."
Dead?

Where only death alone could make the best of their lives, they themselves should contribute a great deal to it. After all, it was a matter of their own *happiness*.

"How dead are the dead really?"

The dead should be asked—but they do not answer, not even very old friends; they are mute, as if they were totally offended or had always been dead; incomprehensible; they do not know anybody; they do not want to know anybody. *As if all dead people were fish.*

Nothing happens.

But life changes, changes in death.

Happy?

And what is *happiness* like?

Disgusting. Inhuman. Greasy. Dirty. Black. Dark. Tumorous. Abraded by the devil. Deflowered. Degraded. Dishonored. Filthy. Disgraceful. Like a house of cards. Two-edged. Like the wind. A fart. Agitating. The worthy reproduction of what is bad. Depriving. Seductive. Intoxicating and poisonous. Vomited. Spit-covered. Promising. Deceitful. Promise-breaking. Sickening. Playful. Idolatrous. Blasphemous. Barefoot. Shivering. Gray-in-gray. Malignant. A curse. Violent. Sinister. Senseless. Shattering. Moody. Contemptuous. Selective. Insensitive. Leaking. Unstable. Greedy. Hoarding. Hypocritical. Attractive. Treasonous. Blind with tears. Rotten. Mudlike. Shit. Turned on. Destructive. Unhappy. Unfriendly. Deceptive. Reflecting recalcitrance. Biting into the right ear. Awkward. Sinful. Dilapidated. Unreal. Sanctimonious. Upsetting. Destructive to the structure. Sneaky as a cat. Constraining. Annoying. Miserly. Something that castrates contentedness. Worse than you think. Evil.

Unkind. Humiliating. Desperately offended. Not beautiful. Hellish. Sensual. Tasteless. Poor (Wretched). Monetary. Expensive. Cheap. Stinking. Terrible. Beastly. Hopeless. Threatening. Pretending to be. Itchy. Large-eyed. Full of empty speeches. Accidental. Painful. Lost bliss. Intoxicating. Vexed. Charming. Finished. Not acquired. Smelly. Loud. Noisy. Loudly noisy. Stale-tasting. Bellowing. Fraud. Predatory fear. Uneasy. Fearful. Consumptive. Dark. Desolate. Bad. Broken. Violated. Yellow illness. Completely repulsive. A barren doe. Exceedingly unfruitful. And in spite of that aroused.

"Official-naglike."
"Legal-paragraph-riderlike."

The dependant bailiffs almost never spoke of filthy happiness. Their worthless salaries choked them. The rope bit into the flesh and tore bloody gashes. The same rope wrapped itself mercilessly around the hearts of the submissively servile "human beings." There it crossed over itself several times and avoided the necessity of one or several knots by weaving a single loose loop into the hemp. Those who were tied up had grown accustomed to it. The officials were pale in the face; the rope blocked their entire blood circulation, even to their brains, and calmed all objections that a thinking mind would have put into words. (Here the word was at neither the beginning nor the end.) The fetter grasped at throat and heart and tied the soul shut. Not a single scab was visible. Blood flowed continually. It could not be stopped.

The subdued workers almost choked to death on the lack of money. They could not keep their families above water. Children drowned in their illnesses. The father did not have the necessary money to buy medicine. The dwelling holes (usually in the basements of the buildings) were damp; that is why the children became ill. Then they were laid out for days in the living room. The parents could find nobody who would loan them a completely worm-eaten wooden coffin for the funeral. When the dead person was finally bedded down in the casket, he stank through and through. The freshness of the flesh was marred by rottenness. The home wallowed in stench. The sparsely visible visitors who came to give their condolences ate the family's last supplies of food. Then they starved. All of them.

For the most part innocent girls died. Boys were fatter, therefore more robust and thievish—now and then (that means always) they stole themselves something to gobble down. As strictly as possible, the bailiffs prohibited their children from stealing—after all, they (that is to say, the bailiffs) were the lowest bearers of justice, the foundation stones of truth.

No wonder the court messengers were constantly in a bad mood and in their dejection thrashed a defendant here and there. They let the cudgels, which they carried hidden, dance across his bent back and struck him until he was ill. It had even happened that some minor bailiff had urinated lukewarmly into the pants pocket of someone who was waiting.

The bailiffs and court summoners were not the only ones who fared badly. Gradually the prison attendants began to use the word "revulsion" even for their dirty work. That is also how they felt while at work, revolting: You rummage through the perforated and possibly wet pants pockets of some person and in so doing get your fingers dirty and moist. Then you put this wretched figure with the holes in his wet pants into a hole and lock the heavy door. Later you ask him a few stupid questions, direct ridiculous and untenable reproaches at him, accuse him, and scratch at his jacket collar like a dog. After that you drag him up before the city, no longer speak to him (you are, after all, offended), and finally you bash his head in, bury him perfunctorily, and simply leave without a word.

Revulsion. Revolting revulsion. Most revolting man.

So much revulsion is forced upon them that after a certain period of time they are already too weary to feel loathing.

Whistling, sticking out their tongues, and the slide-down-my-back-and-brake-at-the-bottom-with-your-tongue feeling ended for them, those miserable beasts.

The Sunday of these men looked different than that of the judge, the prosecuting attorney, and the stenographer. It was burdened with much work as well as being blessed with a bit of money and little food.

The messengers worked on Sundays for merchants or tavern owners; some of them labored as farmhands for farmers near town. They worked harder on Sundays than all the rest of the week. On Monday they were happy to be able to gather new strength. They worked with revolting pleasure. They thirsted for variety. In their ravenous hunger for work, they got calluses.

The women could not work, most of them were ill and long since incapable of sexual intercourse, the children too weak. But not only physical illness gained ground. The sickness of the moral disposition bore large fruit. They generally asked themselves who had sown it. The fertilizer must have been good.

Priests found it not worth the effort to throw a helping glance into those peripheral sections of humanity. They would rather amuse themselves with women whom they degraded to the lowest level on Sundays during their sermons. As soon as they lay upon them breathing heavily, everything was forgotten. They even whispered tenderly in their ears that they were the very best.

Not a word was said about the destroyed lives of the court myrmidons. They did not touch that subject. No poet could be found who *sang about* this misery that nobody wanted to *talk about*. In these peripheral areas every creative manifestation died in embryo. Printed paper was at most wiped across the ass after shitting—or it was not.

The workers worked. The sick girls crouched around alone. Unsympathetically, their parents demanded from them that they move their sick bodies as if they were healthy. Nobody attempted to acknowledge the pain. Meanly, the hale and hearty ones displayed their health against them. They were not hurt by this illness. Thin as a rail, the girls sat before the public and became even thinner. They would have gobbled up food if they had only become aware of a scrap. People from the most populated part of the city bumped against them fatly in their activity—no apology, not the slightest sympathy. The weak body was flung to the floor and trembled hotly—in fever. The empty blood shot violently back and forth.

They remained lying in the gutter for a long time—sometimes dead. *One less mouth. A plug falls out. A life renounces for itself the hope for future happiness.*

The well-to-do people walked on without hesitation. They were not taking a stroll, their walking was work and time was money. (That is why they were always in such a hurry.) If they swindled somebody good, in doing so they tasted their own desire and satisfaction, which more or less wonderfully intoxicated them.

They did not stop to blush with shame over their entire faces. Their faces did not grow red. Indifference fit them well. They were *fond* of themselves and nobody else. They *fond*led themselves. They belonged to themselves. They worshiped themselves. In devotion, they remembered themselves. They sanctified themselves. And denied themselves nothing. They consciously held their own fate in their hands. Now and then they picked up something else.

They bent down over their own abyss. The door into doom stood wide open. Sufferings and shame were foreign to them. They did not experience dizziness when they wandered close along the abyss. They had no fear of entering the chamber of ruin. In high spirits, they faced things boldly . . .

In spite of everything they were poor: They had neither fear nor places that were dear to them. No book that was dear to them. Nothing.

They and their halfway-flattering smiles would never remain the victors—*in the late afternoon hours of humanity, their evening will fall; it will still send them a devilish storm as a greeting.* They will die off.

The high people will stumble over their own feet. The simple people will be washed ashore to live.

A half-suppressed laugh will herald the new era. The dead were buried at an unknown depth. Those sentenced to death scantily buried. A dog whose nose grubbed around a little bit found the scraped body. Nauseated, he turned away—the dog. *He has had enough of human beings.*

The judges buried the world's happiness and justice, not the offenders. A wrong sentence that was carried out could not be corrected by any human hand.

Indeed, the people liked to whisper about legal mistakes that (supposedly) were not simply isolated cases on the agenda. Inconsistencies, they whispered. And how they muttered. More and more. And louder and louder.

Judges conquered their own blushing in the presence of strange bodies. A deed was done—a guilt was punished. A human being sinned—penance was imposed upon another. Justice consisted in the fact that it—justice—usually punished threefold.

The act of punishing was enjoyed. A noose was placed around the neck of a man who had been sentenced to death, who was supposed to be hung. Executioners held him tightly on the rope and dragged him to the place of execution.

He followed silently. Not a single word of opposition was heard.

The image of his dead mother pressed itself before his eyes, which stared out into the world for the last time, brimming with tears. He was the oldest son. She had gotten along well with him, since she liked to hear his friendly words, and not last of all because she had painfully witnessed his coming into the world.

He was an entity whom these professional killers intended to brutalize in a few moments.

He had become a burden to mankind. The court threw him down, to the floor, he became the fodder of *nothingness*. His life span had been exceeded. He would be put to no further use. His miserable personality would be robbed of its body. They would defile his remains.

His body was now only an inducement.

He would be depersonalized.

Last of all they would hit him on the head.

Earlier he had not experienced a single physical feeling, but rather several different feelings of fear.

They cut the rope. And the body fell with a splat into the mud.

The body fell like shit into snow.

The legs became entwined. The stinking stockings on his feet were his only clothing. Only those pieces of underwear had been left to him, so that he would make a funny impression.

His body finally became stiff. He was in a *condition*. He was dead. Without prospect of living longer.

The dead man lay in the mud.

The scared-to-death moments and fractions of moments belonged to the past.

When the condemned man found himself in the most serious gasping for breath of his short life, the beastly executioners broke out into insane laughter that resounded madly from the strong gallows.

The rope quickly went tight around his neck, which broke in no time at all.

It was a hard conflict. *(Death fought with life.)*

His heart pounded furiously, then it was suddenly deathly still.

His hastily searching gaze became glassy.

The hands, which only shortly before had curled around the rope, fell limply away from the body.

Between the cheeks of his butt a little bit of shit:

Death.

The last confession of the condemned man.

Before he had to die, he still had much to say. Nobody wanted to listen to him. He was the outcast. The canker of society. The festering ulcer in the flesh that was otherwise healthy.

He still wanted to speak before he had to give up his body. *But in those last moments the deepest longing to speak encountered the severest speechlessness.* He had to think.

"*I, a human being, was born to die.*

"I will never understand the fact that some people simply flee into death. There is also little time left to me now for that. People who kill themselves disgust me.

"I always wanted to live.

"My mother, a simple woman, gave birth to me in poverty. In a barn. I uttered my first cry in the manure. It escaped from the stall into the deceitful air. The stench of life touched me from the first moment on. My mother did not offer me her own breast. I sucked at the udder of a pregnant cow. The animal essence flowed warmly into me. Suddenly the cow struck out at me. My mother came to herself again, fouled in the animal's urine. The cow hurled me far out.

"Soon after that, my mother wrapped me in ragged swaddling clothes. The last washing of the coarse material had to lie far in the past. My skin was chafed raw. Blood seeped from small wounds. Water flowed between my legs. Far down on my back, everything was black, dirty, and smeared. Meconium. *My faced drowned in tears.* In the biting air, my breath wanted to stop. Just in time the people of the house brought me into the living room. There they examined me in detail. They found birthmarks and no deformities. They liked to exaggerate.

"As I grew up I was sad. Covered with mud and unloved. Nobody gave me love. My mother was taken away from me. Once I wished that she would die.

"In the children's community, I was the lowest. In spite of that, I often laughed halfway flattered when they called me by my name. My birthplace was flooded with little, dirty houses. It was a dusty village. A hole without equal. In the lavatory of the inn sinful things were scratched into the bare wall. Sexual intercourse often occurred there. The sketched atrocities (completely hideous things) were not disturbing, but at most arousing. Rotten and half-naked figures presented themselves stretched out to wanton view. People emptied their swollen bladders incidentally.

"During this time I became an adult. Uneasily, everyone held dominion over my unhealthy spirit. My relationship to others became slavish. I was turned into a stranger. Cold sweat ran in small drops down my bald forehead. People of the same age celebrated their happiness in front of me. Carefully they plowed badness into me. The seed came up and bore plenty of fruit. I began to read and to hate. In the writings I finally found myself again: the spicy and fat and young person with soft and rosy flesh.

"With the courage of despair I rebelled against the horridly raw injustice. With eyes wide open, I saw only unjust conditions far and wide. A false world. A deceptive order. *Nowhere a god.*

"In bed I tossed to and fro. The weight of my whole soul rested heavily upon my body. It threatened to crush me. Illness pressed into my mourning eyes. I became blind to beauty and deaf to sensuality. I was no longer a person.

"My bowed head was snobbish. I rested my elbows on a dreadful world. Uselessly I worked my future into the past. They pushed me from one time into another. I maintained the few ties that I had. I was branded an animal.

"My face shines into the countenance of death."

He had thought those last words with a laugh. Now he became serious, so serious that his eyes grew dark.

"I am a disposable human being. An innocent child I was. The world disconcerted me.

"One day I was arrested by two thin men who were wearing street clothes. This is not intended as a confession. I am not aware of any guilt on my part.

"For that reason they will kill me.

"They will kill me like a criminal.

"I will die like a man."

With these meaningful thoughts he closed his mental confession and surrendered himself to the deathly silence that had settled all around him.

Death came quickly. He stole into that body with a whisper. He was almost ashamed to let this man die miserably, but he had been terrorized into killing. The decision was made without his consent. Death washed his hands in the curdled blood of the man who had been born to die.

The last confession of the condemned man.
No indictment.

Shyly the rushing special messenger came running to the place of execution. In the first moment he saw the lifeless eyes of the man who already lay dead on the ground. In his own excrement. Ridiculous and filthy.

The time that passed was somehow fateful. Nobody wanted to disturb the dead man's peace with his first word. It was too late anyway; nevertheless the messenger wanted to carry out his assignment. He brought the message that they should not have been permitted to hang the defendant, because his guilt was—yes, he said: was—too insignificant for death.

Among them was nobody who could bring him back to life. All of them were only masters of the cruel trade of killing. "As far as I'm concerned, one human being should be permitted to kill another human being only when he can also bring him back to life. (Not before, and even much less after.)"

The messenger grew dizzy. Morally he stepped away. He had never before seen so much human coldness; he shivered quite appropriately. After the messenger had broken the silence, the executioners immediately began to argue. They balled their fists because of the deceased man's clothing.

The condemned man had been hanged almost completely nude. A loincloth was wrapped around his genitals—a stinking rag that the executioners put on all of the defendants and into which the condemned simply spurted their last bodily excreta—urine and excrement and sweat—in their fear.

The executioners could not agree about dividing up the rags. It was customary to divide them up. In the process, it usually came to violent fights that resulted in bloody heads. They tore the clothing—in the fist fight. Nobody managed to get hold of a decent piece. Every advantage came to nothing. Bashed heads were the only perceptible result. From the flat noses trickled blood, snot, and blood again.

At first the man who had brought the news had grown speechless. When he found words again, he spoke sentences that the uneducated killers did not understand.

"The laws are elastic clauses!" he announced seriously and meant something like this: *A holiday approximates a Sunday.* He had never

imagined how quickly you could snuff out a life if you simply wanted to. *"A murder is really no big thing!"*

The man who had spiritually stepped away wanted nothing more to do with this court. He walked out. Angrily, he wanted to give a man standing next to him a good slap in the face; at the last instant he absorbed most of the force of the blow while it was still in the air—as the slap fell. He reined in force. Gently he brushed his hand across the "person's" left cheek. Then he walked quickly away. Onto the street. There he was received by *the normal world.* Everything began anew.

In the future he intended to struggle against the legal system. He set himself the goal of finding the roots of injustice and destroying them.

Previously he had had no ear for unanswered questions, now the number of unresolved ones increased. Not until now had he learned more about life and about the court.

A joy, a harmony, an understanding—once shattered—is difficult to glue back together. It becomes lost—forever. Now he too had learned that happiness is a deceptive thing.

Something still held him back, otherwise he would have taken his own life and would have rushed into death, which greets everyone with open arms who seriously sets about ending his life. He was a serious human being. The death of a stranger and an allegedly guilty man—one could practically say: allegedly innocent man—touched him from out of the dark side of life.

After leaving the court, the former court employee became free for justice—the Palace of Justice had embarrassed him. He did not seek another position in a court. He did not believe that another court would be more receptive to honest law.

He was determined to fight against any charge that might be made against him someday. He had sworn to himself that he would never let himself be condemned by an unjust judge. If he ever broke this solemn oath, he intended to take the greatest liberty—suicide.

Of course, his absolute health would be lost in death. Any sick person would be happy to find it. Now he could only become happy in justice; for him there was no other measure. He wanted what was greatest.

To the bailiff as a human being, his mind promised complete and unconditional confederate loyalty. His brain was the motivating force that called upon him to carry out swift, hard, and determined actions. In its deepest and darkest corner he thought of a one-and-only redeeming state of lawlessness. The question of whether or not his body was in suitable condition did not matter to his mind. The more important question of whether or not lawlessness is the means to achieve equality, justice, and truth, did not spring up. In the face of world history he discarded his guilt with a shrug of his shoulders.

He had become a free-lance revolutionary.

He did not consider that at the very first illegal step the little guardians of the law would decide to take official action and would imprison him. On the other hand, they did not know his intentions.

Actually, he accepted the demands of his mind, but recommended thoughtful deliberations that he held while in bed, and over which he fell asleep too soon. He wanted to go to war against fraud. His lack of knowledge and experience would yet turn out to be a handicap.

The declaration of war that he extracted from himself after all, following long hesitation, was directed against the world. He wanted to change everything fundamentally and not rest until the world spoke of a (his) peace treaty of victory.

He wanted to be a decisive factor in the war.

If he were to proceed against himself logically, he would have to declare war against war itself, and not only against the war that would pose other questions and set other tasks in addition to those that already existed for him.

His moral balance was now upset once and for all, without his knowing it. Through the destruction of his morality he lowered his own humanity.

With respect to his own person, he coldly avoided every authority to which he was subordinate. He intended to resolve personal conflicts during inner struggles (attacks)—accompanied by sharp thought discordances whose cranial revenge was a bad headache.

First he strengthened himself in the eyes of his few acquaintances, but without forgetting the executioners who bashed each other's heads in while dividing up clothing.

Later his attacks were more public and attracted more attention.

Finally he was able to learn where the chief executioner lived. The obvious fact that the latter wore the dead man's pants, which the executioner's wife made wearable again by patching them together with laboriously detailed and minutely tedious work, drove him quite mad. Then one day he picked up the gun that he had acquired in the meantime and took the executioner's filthy life with a well-aimed shot into his violently pounding heart. His breath rattling, the executioner lay on the floor, a piece of meat that called death to mind. He had died like a coward, although he had already so often *been permitted* to stare into the dying eyes of others.

As coarsely funny flesh and blood, the executioner began to stink and annoyed the passers-by with his repulsive odor.

That was the justice of the former bailiff who was supposed to be arrested by the most subordinate of all civil servants. Even before the guardian of the law finished his little memorized arrest statement, *the murderer out of justice* swallowed poison and departed more heroically than his victim from a life that had lately horrified him.

In the cemetery for people who commit suicide, where they also buried the dead dogs and cats, he found his final resting place. A place without rest. Another executioner held his bare ass over the grave of the murderer and suicide victim and let steaming shit plop down upon it—that was his revenge. A stray cat sniffed at it and placed some of its bodily waste next to it.

That is how he ended. Nobody wasted a word on his person. He was dead—forever. *Had died namelessly.*

He had not changed the world—it had changed him, but also only a little. What was one more dead man in *this* world?

J. Purch, Peter F., and Miss Lauschig had spent a Sunday. It had become Monday for them. They hurried to get to the court.

It was a Monday on which all of them, Purch, F., and Miss Lauschig, could say for the first time that they had no more "work." All of the legal cases had been resolved *one* way or the other—now they stood there, there before the void, carrying on meaningless activities. After all, they had to work. They were not *over*paid for nothing.

The first one who recognized this state of suspension was the prosecuting attorney. He made his realization consequential for everyone by saying: "We have no work! None at all! We must do some work! But we no longer have any work! For that reason, we will do *some* work!"

Over the faces of the court employees came a vespertine relaxation that usually did not set in until late afternoon.

That is how the court was; it had hired people upon whom it could impose no work. It found itself in a serious dilemma. On the one hand, it could only remedy the lack of work for the prosecuting attorney, the judge, and the stenographer by promoting crimes, atrocities, or at least the poisoning of wells, and on the other hand it had to take into strict consideration that *the fewer* leisure-time murderers, lechers, and destroyers of nature there were, *the better*. A way out into some kind of employment had to be found. *"Employment."* They had to discover a side street, the judge thought. (The stenographer was silent because she had nothing to say.) Suddenly every comment was meaningful.

In order not to humiliate themselves completely, they at least has to pretend to have work—but that was no way out, no side street. All of them searched strenuously for some kind of work.

For the first time it became very clearly apparent: When given their autonomy, the officials were not very imaginative. Their dearth of ideas overgrew the steadily descending steps of consternation. They felt alarm (not only down the spine). A feeling of weakness crept into their bodies, and a feeling of dizziness that made the world spin, into their heads. Official objectivity drowned in the flood of these feelings. From the deeply reflecting minds of the servants of the law rose mental smoke that only gradually dissipated. *The smoke of their agony.* Their minds were so confused that in terror they forgot the morning newspaper. Wildly and fretfully they lost all respect for themselves.

It was no misfortune, but a piece of good luck that did not cost anybody his life, for: once they "worked," it was at least one life's turn to end. They were above the dusty ruined wasteland that developed in the family after the death of their relative. *And louder and louder the relatives then said that they had lost their "best part."*

What humiliation, suddenly to sit stuck to their chairs without work and bore holes in the air of the law office! "What degradation!"

A mental flash of lightning went through the prosecuting attorney's mind. J. Purch had the solution. After all, he was an inventor.

"I shall bring charges in an invented, assumed case. I'll draw up the indictment in the best possible manner. The stenographer will write down everything and submit it to the judge. The judge will then pronounce sentence concerning the case. We will, as we have always done, pass the condemned man on and turn him over to the law.

"It will become a just judgment. The most just ever. The defendant's utterances will not disturb us in any way, because there won't be any. For the first time we will peacefully indict, record, and judge in the *most* just fashion!"

Peter F. and Miss Lauschig abandoned themselves to a momentary dizziness of joy, which soon passed, and they began to work, to employ themselves. They went, so to speak, into action. "Into the middle of it."

J. Purch sat down behind his enormous wooden prosecuting attorney's desk and organized his professional instruments, which were similar to those of the judge: an iron cross that rested on a copper hemisphere, two silver-plated candlesticks with the lard-white contents of two halfway burned-down candles, a box that was three-fourths full of matches for lighting the flame on the wick of the wax stick, writing materials and other objects—enormously important for the just determination of truth.

The prosecuting attorney cleared his throat twice rather loudly, the first time in the stenographer's direction, the second time, looking at the judge. Then he began speaking in a failing voice. Finally he succeeded. He spoke. He dictated. Miss Lauschig sat there mentally calm and had long ago moved her fingers into position. Impatiently sliding around in the threadbare armchair, she waited for lofty prosecuting-attorney words. During his dictation she repeatedly looked at his lips in order to read different words from them. Miss Lauschig was accustomed to his speeches, she put nothing wrong on paper, although she sometimes scribbled furiously and scratching sounds came from the writing instrument.

Meanwhile, the judge either read or ate up Miss Lauschig with his greedy eyes. Perhaps he was thinking about some (theatrical) play. He did not want to criticize anyone—not at all. Nor did he wish for any criticism or examination of himself by others.

Several times he seemingly casually picked up the tulip-shaped glass of water that stood on his desk, moved it to his mouth that had become dry as he read, and tipped it when it was as high as his lips. Trembling water played around his teeth and ran deeper into his body. He held back and did not drink often. The drops that splashed on his shirt were called water spots the next day. Thereby, attentive people recognized that he did not change his shirt.

Meanwhile, the prosecuting attorney composed the indictment in a single stream of words. He did not restrain his tongue from speaking until everything was ready and could be looked at as a truly finished document: *"With date. With stamp. With signature and number."*

The sins that he blamed on an unknown person could have been committed by himself. J. Purch filed charges concerning personal experiences that disquieted him.

In his thoughts, Purch was still looking for a starting point, and after that a connecting point to begin and go on with the indictment. He took heart and was no longer himself but entirely the prosecuting attorney. Closing his eyelids, he withdrew from the influence of his environment. Then he folded his arms. For the most part, he dictated blindly.

Miss Lauschig still listened to him even long after he had become silent. The silence was disconcerting to her. If the prosecuting attorney started speaking again, it was as if someone freed his stomach of gas in a public meeting.

In his capacity as prosecuting attorney, Purch was certainly not narrow-minded . . ., but very narrow-minded. His indictment was carefully worked out—as an inventor he was a compulsive quibbler—and overstrained. It spoke of disillusioned and disillusioning affection, of quickly and violently passing pain of life, of general revulsion, of pressing family difficulties, of menopause, of the sick society into which the pathogenic defendant hardly found his way, of excessive fear of the world, and of suspicions that arose beneath the drops of prosecuting-attorney sweat. Wet, sweaty, and relaxed, he showed the evidence of crime. His opinions about the blame were irrefutable, nobody dared offer the slightest objection. J. Purch became completely involved in his death-bringing work. He knew that there were still too few laws and many of them with flaws. The most severe punishment that many laws administered was *only* LIFE IMPRISONMENT. He cursed that, as was appropriate for a prosecuting attorney. He, he said, would be incapable of judging on the basis of such a law.

It was not his first dictated composition of charges to be placed before the court, and it was under no circumstances the worst or even the last. In point of language, it could be handed to the judge without hesitation: Under the effect of his daring expressions, other points of view could be rejected. The judge was amazed at each new one, although he had to reckon with sharply-worded sentences again and again.

"If it please the High Court!

"I accuse. And I accuse sharply. Most sharply."

Purch ordered the stenographer not to mark the ends of the last sentences with exclamation points (!) because he wanted to exclude any suspicion of an upsurge of feeling. He claimed to be knowledgeable and officially reserved. No inner motivation could divert him from a determination of truth that was just and acceptable to the court—and that in every one of his many cases; *"he sat tight in the saddle. No horse, no matter how obstinate, could throw him off."*

Then he was bent upon moving on in the lattice-work of sentences. He dictated everything even more quickly—almost cold and untouched, caressed solely by the law.

"His deeds will bring the defendant a bloody destiny. Without core or substance he will proceed from the indictment to the judgment. Calculating speeches do not render me (more) harmless. The process will inescapably come to its conclusion because only the accusation brings about the indictment and the indictment the judgment.

"Even before the last of my deductions, the condemned man will coarsely curse his maker, which the prosecution must immediately take into consideration. Not only probability, but also real evidence testifies that with abusive words and jokes that were directed at them the accused insulted the officials who arrested him by order of the court. He did not apologize; such manners are completely foreign to him.

"The fact that the accused sings pleasantly has no bearing at all upon the passing of judgment, if for no other reason than because the prosecuting attorney is not in good singing voice.

"His lies and daydreams are immense. His observations, sick. In a preliminary investigation for the indictment, I had to realize that such people literally outdo themselves in their horrible wickedness.

"Further, on the basis of my tests, I recognized in these homeless people an unjustified but unfathomable hatred of courts and justice. They spontaneously resist any justice. My conclusions are not general observations. I composed my opinion based upon the human object—it is correct, and the punishments to be derived from it must be applied to the same thing.

"The circumstance of the guilty man's social climb is noteworthy and very helpful to the judge. Like the forefathers of many people, the defendant's ancestors were poor peasants and lazy laborers whose meager possessions led them to theft, fraud, and poaching. Their crimes have still not been expiated. Their descendant inherited all of the captured goods as sole heir; therefore he must take on the punishment that befits these deeds. If he recognizes his guilt on the basis of his own insight, the amount of punishment can be reduced somewhat. A morbid refusal to view the guilt as his own must be combated and melted down in the acknowledgment of guilt.

"His ancestors' plunder, which is not inconsiderable, will be confiscated and sold for the general welfare of the people.

"If the condemned man is married, then all of the circumstances suggest that it was not a marriage based on love. The groom married out of selfishness, in order to obtain the wealth of his bride, who was somewhat older than he. She was happy to get hitched, as the popular saying goes, and blindly ignored that fact. (Love blinds, according to another aphorism from the same parlance.)

"Even on the basis of these points, the man who stands before the court is guilty, although these are his most insignificant crimes.

"The fact that he raped his wife during their wedding night is no crime, it is more a punishment for the marital duties that the woman did not fulfill.

"Even smaller are the transgressions that the father commits against his children, if such emerge from the aforementioned marriage. Blows and curses directed at his daughters and sons have too little force to be recognized as such by the court.

"In his youth he violated the unwritten law. He neglected his parents' small-animal holdings and their bee culture. He did not appear at the funeral of his grandfather, who fell to the ground dead after a brawl in the village tavern.

"Although he was taught about everything in school, he revolted dangerously against his teachers. He tripped them and wet their chairs with his exposed penis.

"When—in defiance of the teachers—his crafty activities became more irritating, he was forced to leave the school. He began to work—and to think: *He doubted the immaculateness of a Virgin and Mother of God.* His questions became more and more impertinent and challenging.

"The defendant undoubtedly slithered on the fringe of society. Nevertheless, he wore tailored suits made of expensive cloth, which he changed after short intervals of time. Nothing could dull his effusive enthusiasm for the taste of the time.

"*That alone would be indictment enough.*

"The excuse that he is young and that every young person is an imaginable instance of iniquity must not be listened to, especially not before the court, which has to *find* the whole truth and nothing but the truth, and if nothing else works, must *invent* it.

"The motivating forces that had a great effect did not surprise him because he had been waiting for them since childhood. With exaggerated sensitivity, he surrendered himself to the enjoyment of life. In all situations. He could completely succumb to the enchantment of an exaggerated state of intoxication.

"He abrogated the time-honored manners. That is hostile. Antagonistic toward all.

"He treated his female bedmates well. After dealing with them once on the white sheets, he let them go. They had expected more. An enduring bond. Seldom have we seen women who were so broken with pain and so sorrowful. And seldom such really young ones.

"Not that I am jealous, but: *That alone would be indictment enough.*
"His view of the world was desolate—it was his own fault.
"That alone would be indictment enough.
"The punishment would be great.
"One proof of his sins is the constant unemployment to which he surrendered himself, and which he himself evoked by yawning in the business owner's face while being introduced, and by severely reviling him—after the latter had reproved him.
"That alone would be indictment enough.
"Therefore, concerning the defendant, I can say that he is felonious, incapable of living among people, and ruined. It is not only I who must recognize this social derogation, since the condemned man has become acquainted with it. The judge must critically examine this almost standard diminution. And pass judgment.
"This defendant personifies true evil, and he is proud of it. He carries his nose higher than other people. With this claim, however, I do not intend to suggest that he is unusual; I simply intend to say that other people are more ordinary.
"That alone would be indictment enough.
"Still, even after these enumerations of his crimes, the defendant has the impudence not to feel like an outcast and a failure.

"My patience is slowly becoming exhausted.

"At last justice will have the duty to open its mouth.

"His existence will finally be placed in question. That question will afflict him with the suffering of being unsuitable for life.

"The accused is neither blameless before the law nor pure before his own filthy conscience—he must be condemned.

"I must point out one more thing here: It was not the court that came to the condemned man—the condemned man came to the court—or at least his guilt pleaded for a just punishment. Our court has enough pride not to run after criminals.

"The judgment will be a formative experience for him. It will give him a different physical condition.

"The condemned man is no longer a drifting man; following my indictment, he is a driven man.

"If it please the High Court!

"I request the death sentence *for* the defendant. In his entire life he has attained to no mitigating circumstances."

The prosecuting attorney concluded with those words. The stenographer placed the final punctuation mark (.) on the letter-smeared paper and gave the document to J. Purch for his signature. He wrote his name with wispy, illegible strokes on the bottom part of the document. The prosecuting attorney kept a copy for himself; it was very mangled because the carbon copy had not turned out well. Miss Lauschig gave this first transcription to the judge for perusal and definitive passing of judgment.

Peter F. accepted it—poking fun at it—but not without having slapped the stenographer tenderly on her taut behind. She thought to herself: *"If somebody slaps you on the left buttock, turn the right one to him,"* and transformed her thoughts into gestures that bore slapping fruit.

The judge immediately devoted his entire close attention to the papers. He bent low over them, and several times he had a very sad and distinctly thoughtful expression—that was the first sign that he gave when he was considering passing a death sentence without possibility of appeal.

Such a sentence was always on his mind. According to his conception of justice it was the only just one.

After he had apparently ended his examination—he rose and strolled to the window—slowly and deliberately he pronounced the sentence.

His verdict was final and did not tolerate the slightest objection. Nobody had the power to lessen the force of his judgment. He tied everyone's hands.

To the stenographer, who had the thought that she could not escape writing at all any more, he spoke with a strangely throaty voice.

This situation of the prosecuting attorney and the judge working hand in hand had something fateful and even fatal about it.

"If it please the High Court!

"I am disgusted with this scoundrel, carnal seducer, subverter, fraud, sex murderer, and intruder into human society. It will give me no pleasure to condemn this person. He is a pig who transgresses against everything. This being, this deceitful, miserable, pitiful, extremely suspicious, depraved, and repulsive being must be destroyed. I could spit. If I had vomited, it would turn my stomach again. This person is without equal and a failure. It is terribly, unpleasantly touching: The criminal shamelessly faces me like a rake, and when he is led out of the courtroom, he does not make the slightest effort to face me instead of turning his back toward me. It does not matter that the accused is not present; if he were here, he would go out the door, turning his back to me. He can therefore be certain of my dislike; nevertheless I shall be just and shall not impose a more severe punishment upon him than is at all possible. His carnal nature has no right to live in the human throng. He is a unique example of depravity. He stubbornly persists in it without the suggestion of the slightest attempt to better himself or to let himself be improved. Any attempt would be in vain and a failure; any investment of energy, spirit, and thoughts would soon prove to be a waste, because he is unreceptive to that which is good. He has severely sinned, according to the words: He who is not with us is against us! Nobody can dispossess him from this crushing burden because the masses pardon nothing; they fly, as vultures fly to cadavers, except that they do not plunge down onto decaying bodies but onto any little human trespass. Even the tiniest flaw produces the criminal, the murderer, and the culprit. He destroyed his miserable life himself. He is therefore a suicide. I shall pronounce the most just verdict of which I have ever been or ever shall be capable. *The only soothing thing that I can say about him is that he is sad.* I could add things infinitely, but he must be nailed down on what he has done wrong and be crucified on the law. He must be condemned. The voice of his own conscience must pound it into the defendant whom I do not know, that he indulged in vice and culpable misery like a wild swinish creature—his crimes ran pleasantly over his body, even though he was no implement of mood but a human being who longed for and craved them. He wanted to experience the pleasant feeling of a (his) deed, vividly and plastically, and contacted the injured parties with his hands. He exposed his desire. He produced anxiety. This anxiety producer and fear creator! The court will seek the truth that enthuses from the depths, and sling it almost maliciously and arrogantly at the defendant—at least it will appear that way—although the pronouncement of sentence will have a cold effect. The fact that he infuriated us does not injure us further. He was a scourge to the people, one who struck at them like a polypod with a thousand arms and spread naked fear. Only isolated couples saved themselves from the madness of insane fear. Left to his own devices, a human being would not venture to struggle against the bitterness that he created. With all severity, his reign of tyranny and fear crammed people into the prison of confused fear. The sufferings produced an agitation like that experienced in the times of the great revolutions and wars, when man was still subjugating the earth, and later, when he wanted to obtain all happiness by force. The scoundrel is lazy, repulsive, disgusting, and indolent; I loathe him because he systematically became sexually excited in order to be sexy; he discharged his murderous, unnatural instinct, egotism, and selfishness together, carnal shamelessness in *the sweet tumult* that degenerately and miserably loudly accompanied his heavenly ecstasy and his rapture. He must pay dearly for his subjugation of everything that is nice. He committed offenses against many people. He threw that which is noble into the dirt. Even in the pool of blood he was devilishly crude. The number of human crews that he dragged into crime is large. Pleasing his palate meant death for innumerable animals. (In the case of chickens, he assaulted their necks directly.) Lost and impoverished, he stands unknown before his just and true judge. It is impossible for him to escape. From now on the court will prescribe his path for him. For him who flagrantly unjustly and sentiently uncomprehendingly hunted and persecuted. Truth forces the hell of the hunted and persecuted upon him, in which he will finally be consumed by fire. Not in a supernatural place, no, human flesh will feast on his pains.

"Injustice and crime will return to his sin-inflamed body that stood before justice with spinsterly timidity. The spectators will enjoy themselves at his death. His pains will give them back the freedom that he stole from them. He will leave their circle. It will be a just punishment. Nobody will ask: Where are you? In the name of the High Court I announce the verdict and spit it at his feet, from where he will lick it up manically, as justice demands.—If it please the High Court! I condemn this carnal calculator of feelings in the name of the High Court, of truth, etc., to kicks and blows on his butt. Two attendant bailiffs will alternate in bashing him. The first with his right foot, which will be in a sturdy shoe, the second with an unplaned wooden club—and they will do that until the strength of their hand or foot gives out and their limbs are completely numb. Obviously, two skilled people will strike. When this punishment has been carried out, the second part will go into force: the death sentence. In the name of everyone, I condemn the recognizedly guilty man to death. My verdict is to have its effect soon. Any appeal is prohibited and illegal.

"Everything must be as though the devil himself had come for him."

The sentence reads exactly that way. *Blows. Punches. Death. And devil.* Miss Lauschig was devoid of any thought. Happy not to have to write any longer, she got up from the warm chair. There now remained only a little pain in the fingers of her writing hand. Then she quickly went to the lavatory. Her bladder plaintively demanded it.

Peter F. leaned back hard in his chair, closed his eyes, and carefully and compassionately kneaded his scalp. He stretched his legs far out in front of him. A crippling emptiness *was a lead weight* on his numb limbs.

Evening slowly came, and they thought more readily of going home. The day's work was finished. (The night shift was already waiting impatiently. *Like a little child.*)

When Miss Lauschig came into the office for the last time that day, she indignantly asked the judge to write his signature beneath the judgment. He refused to obey this "order" and put her off until the next day.

Under no circumstances would Peter F. change the verdict, he simply did not want to do anything, not even sign the paper. The next day he would still give additional instructions that would lead to the execution of the judicial sentence. The next evening he intended to go to the theater. He was always an avid theatergoer. When he visited the theater he dressed well. "He had beautiful shoes. They glowed black into the night. Stockings that did not yet stink. New trousers. Fresh underpants. A pressed and starched shirt. A velvet tie. A dark coat. Gloves and an overcoat. A hat." It was nice to go to the theater.

Before leaving, Miss Lauschig hastily cleaned up the legal office a little bit, put everything in its usual place, aired the place out . . . , then they went home—to the night shift.

J. Purch went to his inventing.

The judge had invited his stenographer to dinner in a dirty cafe in the red-light district. They sat alone in a small room and were voluntarily excluded completely from the happenings in the restaurant. If they wanted something or somebody, they yelled for the waiter. He came into the booth, small, grimy, and reverential, and inquired about the requirements of the lady and the gentleman, as he called his customers. Sweating, smelling bad, and with sore feet, he soon brought what was wanted, most carefully closed the door to the chamber, and quietly left.

The room was low*er*, warm, and stimulating. Paintings with nude couples in the most risqué positions adorned the walls. In front of the windows, curtains in the most disreputable colors hung clear to the floor. The floor was covered with carpet; when walking, one sank approximately two finger-widths into it. A few flowers rounded out the room's square image. In one corner stood large sofas on which people could also lie down without any trouble. They were covered with an undeterminable material that could be removed and replaced easily. In front of the objects for sitting or lying, a large round table loaded with damask and white napkins extended itself broadly. Cutlery, plates, glasses, everything was there. In the middle stood a large lamp that spread soft light, directly above it a redundant chandelier, which, however, hung in the air without a source of electricity. If you looked more closely, you could see that pictures from this very room were drawn on the walls; they were ones in which people made love. "One little appetite after another."

After dinner they went home without making any detours.

Having arrived there, they immediately undressed, Miss Lauschig first; Peter F. was very helpful to her as she took off her clothes. If there was nothing to do at the moment, he watched. His eyes glistened.

With the judge's help, the stenographer had already slipped off her coat in the anteroom.

In the corner of the apartment where they undressed, he always felt like laughing. One day the judge had brought two friends along to the apartment to spend the night. For lack of space, one had to sleep on the bare floor and the other bedded down on an upholstered sofa that was much too short to lie on. In the morning he was so weary from sleeping there that he had to be slapped out of his slumber.

After his brief fit of laughter, she dragged Peter F. longingly into the room, where she unbuttoned her jacket and blouse. Peter F. pulled the two pieces of clothing from her quivering torso. The shoes flew from her feet into the darkest corner of the room. Carefully she pulled her stockings from her legs. Meanwhile, her playmate opened the zipper of her skirt. She pushed it lower and stepped out of the dress with two not overly large steps. Underneath, her white skin glistened. Peter F. still restrained himself.

Now he undressed himself—and was undressed by her. He slipped out of his coat and vest, undid the knot in his tie. Miss Lauschig pulled it from the collar of his shirt. After a short flight, coat, vest, and tie landed on the back of the chair, which was already burdened down with pieces of the stenographer's clothing. Miss Lauschig attended to his shirt buttons, then she pulled the shirt quickly over his head, which significantly assailed his hairdo. After the shirt and undershirt were also lying on the chair, she caressed his hair smooth with the bare palm of her hand. The judge took off his shoes and stockings. The stenographer's grasp, first between his legs and then somewhat higher and more repulsively at his zipper had a little ceremony to it, so that holy-profane feelings tickled the judge. The pant legs slid down his legs to the floor. Miss Lauschig picked the trousers back up, folded them, and draped them over a wooden clothes hanger that she loosely hung by its iron hook on the edge of the wardrobe. (The judge stood there waiting.) After hanging up the trousers, Miss Lauschig quickly swung around toward him on one foot, and with her naked body—her breasts wobbled a little—tried to remove the judge's underpants. That was much easier thought than done. The stiffness of his penis made it difficult to pull them down; therefore she had to pull the upper edge of the pants away from his belly—his sex organ sprang free—only then could she remove the pants from his body. First she inverted them and slipped them over his hairy legs with the upper edge down. Peter F. lifted one foot after the other and climbed out of the pants; with her finger tips, the stenographer threw the pants to the edge of the bedside rug where both of them now remained silent for a while.

As if by chance, Peter F. grasped Miss Lauschig by her upper arms and penetrated her. While standing they moved their bodies as you do in sexual intercourse.

In bed they repeated the pleasant game two or three times.

Peter F. smelled strongly of food spices. Miss Lauschig was bathed in sweat; she fell asleep happily excited. The man was still occupied with thoughts. He shivered. He reached for his underpants, which he caught hold of without having to get out of bed. Awkwardly he put them on his lower body. After a while the call of nature forced him to go to the lavatory, where he remained even after passing water and for the first time asked himself about the meaning of all the things that he pursued. Yes, in his thoughts he used the disgraced word *"pursued."*

Lost in thought he reached once more for his erection, which had already come again. Only when a pitiful squirt resulted from his movements did he recognize what he had done. Softly, he crept quickly into the bathroom and then into bed, wrapped his arms and legs around the sleeping woman's body, and shut his eyes. He began dreaming immediately, to be more precise, about a woman. She was unfamiliar to him, as much a stranger as the defendant upon whom he was imposing his death sentence. The fact that she was making the greatest efforts to castrate him scared him from his sleep. That night he got no more rest next to the quietly sleeping young woman.

Only waking up—early in the morning—gave him relief.

Miss Lauschig refused the good-morning kiss. Unpleasantly touched, Peter F. turned his body away from her. Soon after that, he suddenly jumped out of bed to drink a glass of water.

Both of them began to wash themselves and completed the process extremely carefully because they had completely gone without doing it the night before. They did not conserve the hot water. The soap made decent bubbles.

After washing, they ate. When they had also carried out and completed this vitally necessary process, the judge set out for the court. Before she went to the court, Miss Lauschig removed the sheet from the bed and slid fresh linen over the flowered mattress.

J. Purch, Peter F., and Miss Lauschig arrived at the court before the beginning of working hours.

Early in the morning, Peter F. wrote his signature. He made the death sentence enforceable. With that a human life, or, better said, a human death was sealed.

Miss Lauschig gave the verdict to the appropriate people who carry out every sentence. The sphere of activity of these people was always limited and ended in the quick and painful killing of people who had been sentenced to death. They were masters of several forms of execution, and each was effective in its way, *each yelled into Death's ear; he never ignored the insistent call and reached for life with open arms.*

The executioners could not do much with nothing more than the death sentence. For that reason, right below his (more or less legibly) written-out name, the judge wrote a broadening secondary order, which decreed that the responsible little people had the task of seeking, finding, and killing a person—it was not important whether the person was guilty or innocent—so that the court's judicial decision could be satisfied. *"For everyone is guilty."*

A hint given by the judge said that it would be most sensible to snatch a man from a larger crowd, lead him to the place of execution, and confront him with the truth. Even the very coincidence that he was on the street among people, thus making his arrest possible, almost provoking it, made him severely guilty; only death could compensate for his transgression, the judge recognized.

The senior killer accepted the assignment as if his men had to bring about something small *and not* something greater.

He decided for himself that in the evening two of his subordinates, creeping through the streets like roaming dogs, would take some man or other between them and lead him to the place of execution. They could decide the how of death for themselves, according to their desire.

In his thoughts he designated the two men who would carry it out. Pale, young fellows with dark rings under their eyes and pimples on their faces, who went pale when *their master* condescended to look them straight in the face. The responsible man cursed his workers; any friendly association was out of the question. If it were not necessary to speak to these employees and give them assignments, he would put an end to these humiliation "monologues" immediately. It was a handful that he had to supervise, and he did it to the satisfaction of his mandators, who stood far above him. (Measured against their greatness he was small and insignificant. When the conditions were viewed that way, the executioners, who were employed as killers, were no longer human beings, but animals without will who were used for the dirtiest work.)

These two laboring animals, who were put to work, were degraded masses of flesh with indefinite and indefinable faces. A recollection that was devoted to their meaningless appearance would be wasted.

They were animals because they worked for a salary that one would not at all dare to offer human beings. Their salaries did not increase over the years, although they did their human—or better said: animal—best. These myrmidons and cultivated traitors to humanity were an unparalleled curse.

They always lived in uncertainty, dark spirits, and dejection that made them think back upon beautiful pictures. Although they never in their lives painted a pretty picture with their existence. The sounds that they caused were, to be sure, familiar but stinking. They thought they were creating music but destroyed what was beautiful in the notes, musical instruments, and voices. They had not learned to write. With a devil-may-care attitude, they disregarded fine points in the external form of life. They had never learned that you could also *eat* with a knife. They ate bones clean. The raw chickens crackled in their blood-covered mouths. They were always hungry. *"I could eat up the whole world!"* The first worked with his left hand tickling the cow's face, the strong right hand tore meat from the bloated belly, and the second lay drinking beneath its full udder.

Their narrow-minded consciousness of existence was characterized by worries, pain, hunger, irritation, anger, fury, self-gratification, spit-in-your-face, and no scruples. The inner compulsion toward good had died long ago.

They never took a position and never moved into position.

They were familiar with no contradiction to the idea that they always had to be hungry. "There is nothing at all that is not to be eaten!" they said to themselves. With a jubilant cry of fully contented joy, they sank their teeth into the meat.

In the evening they would kill. (Repulsive.)
Apparently equipped with the necessary tools, they directed their steps into the city's residential center. *("A dark hour of justice dawns.")* With the loud banging of their coarse shoes they intended to stomp the honor of the laws into the mud. Into the swamp. They were men who moved more easily with their legs than with their tongues.

A newly won piece of wisdom would burden them.

Their entire life was concentrated in those hours of the day in which they ground their teeth and filled their bellies.

They were terribly sober and vacuous.

With hungry eyes they looked out into the rest of the sated world.

For them, feelings of solidarity and the smell of kinship were no fragrant ocean full of good things, but a stinking public lavatory that, against better judgment, formed a bond of blood between brother and sister. (They were not animals, but simply human beings.)

It had grown dark; they plunged into the terrors of that night.

They found scraps of food beneath their feet, which their clammy fingers quickly carried to their drooling mouths. Smacking their lips, they choked the garbage down; they did not become nauseated; they did not smell their own bad breath.

For them there was only one pure and unadulterated truth: A human being *had to* be killed.

"Will we see each other tomorrow in the theater?" the average man auspiciously asked a young lady who walked down the outside stairs of the theater beside him.

"An excellent question, which superficially seems to be one, but is only based upon the sexual process as an end in itself. It will be rather difficult for me to answer that niggling question, although you know that I like to go to the theater. Let's wait and see, rather: you wait and see!" she masterfully mouthed at him.

The spell of her words drew him onto the street where the cold bailiffs caught sight of him. Forcefully they encircled his suit-clad body with the raw power of their naked arms. He surrendered himself to this force without resistance! It lifted him from the ground; it seemed to him as though he were floating weightlessly above the street; and he did not know where he was going.

The crowd of people that had surrounded him and the female theatergoer did not concern themselves further about him. They all melted away. He was only a stranger with their passion, the theater. What did they care about the stranger whom nobody here knew?

"You are under arrest!" the bearer on his right warbled in his ear. With a questioning facial expression he leaned his left cheek against the head of the supporter on his left, who gave him no further explanation.

He was under arrest and did not know why. His excellent knowledge of the law did not help at all. He had simply been arrested. He could not remember a crime. For that reason, he reflected carefully and remained in his comical posture. His head was tilted to the side, his hands an entwined unity with the arms of strangers, his torso horribly squashed, his feet drawn up to his body above the ground. The sudden deduction based on his question and his feelings made him afraid. He was empty and felt himself plunging into an abyss. But he did not fall straight down, but flew ahead. He was treated like a tramp, criminal, or someone who had just been arrested.

If he did not *remain* quiet, they promised him, he would receive a blow to the back of his neck. It was a "good" threat, since they only spoke of its possible implementation, but not of its actual realization.

Finally they arrived at a rectangular area that was obviously a place of execution. All four (equally long) sides were lined with killing tools. One side housed a gallows, the other a broad beam to which the condemned person was bound in order to be shot. Across from the gallows was a guillotine, and opposite the firing-squad beam a deep pond had been constructed, into which nonswimmers were thrown. Culprits who were to be strangled were placed in the middle of the execution area, which was flooded with human blood; the blood drain had plugged up a short time ago because the blood in it had coagulated.

When the fatter of the two executioners caught sight of his workplace, he howled merrily into the stillness of the night.

"*Do you hear the silence?*" were the first words of the man in the middle after he had steadfastly remained silent all the way there.

Nobody answered, not even the echo; only the second man gave a shrill whistle.

An "innocent man" was supposed to die in order to comply with the verdict that unemployed legal practitioners had given.

Finally his personal fate began to dawn on the "innocent man," he was to be murdered, sentenced . . .

Others who were condemned to death would now quarrel urgently with their fate. In their despair they would speak senseless words that had fought their way out of the deepest recesses of their souls and nevertheless revealed the truth.

"I despise you who are for the death penalty—and who carry it out blindly. You should be ashamed of your repulsive task! Spit in each other's faces! I do not agree with it! The death penalty is not the medicine that will make your lives healthy, people. By murdering the guilty you do not fight against guilt. Away with the executioners!" he now said.

This prisoner let no more words cross his lips; fascinated, he watched the myrmidons.

They took off their shoes and climbed into boots that stood on one side of the execution area, and which looked even coarser. The footwear was smeared with blood, a few finger-widths high. They would probably pull him to the middle of the square; it was surely for that reason that they put boots on their feet.

When they were finished, they put handcuffs on the silent man, which immediately cut into his flesh. Blood trickled down the backs of his hands. "Drops of blood arouse no sympathy, especially not where it does not exist."

The killers with a court order took off his clothes. They were entitled to the clothes. He had nice shoes. They glistened black into the night. Stockings that did not stink yet. New trousers. Fresh underpants. A pressed and starched shirt. A velvet tie. A dark jacket. Gloves and an overcoat. A hat. The executioner who has previously been bare-headed was already wearing the hat.

Hasty removal of the overcoat, jacket, and shirt had difficulties attached to it because the man who was to be unclothed had his hands bound. The bailiffs briefly removed a part of the fetters and tore the sleeves from his limbs. He felt biting pain. After that they tied him again like an ox that nobody trusts. In addition he was also tethered to a pole. Then he stood there: with the indispensable and simply appropriate loin rag that the hangmen had meanwhile wrapped around his hips with splayed fingers. He was their prisoner; *they could do with him what they wished; they could deal with him as they pleased.*

Tied to the post, he listened to the life-robbers fight over the clothes. For a long time, they could not agree, and for that reason they threw dice for the individual pieces of clothing.

Newly clothed—(the condemned people were not always well-clothed; he was a welcome isolated case)—they moved to the punishment, which they intended to carry out, taking each sentence into consideration. They struck and pounded at him until their limbs gave out. He had been beaten unconscious. A few buckets of water raised him to his feet.

The hitters regarded him as an onerous extraneous element. In different places his skin had broken open. Mistakenly they had also pinched him, spit in his face, and stoned his body. They had beaten him to a pulp, as the "glorious" saying goes. The effectiveness of the blows was painfully unpleasant to him.

When they asked him for his last request, he was certain that it was really a question of death here and not a matter of some bad joke (of his friends). He had no definite wish.

He expressed a kind of longing for *sleepless nightmares at the break of day*, which, however, he dismissed. When he requested the disconnected seduction of three actresses, when he wanted to stare (once more!) at a rotten pig's cadaver, they uncomprehendingly denied him his last right.

But the men who did not comprehend his desire did not want to let him die *that way*, therefore they kneaded his entire body.

After they had put his body through the mill the expression of their strangeness became even stronger. In spite of the cleanliness and orderliness of the new clothes, he regarded them as annoying. The clothes did not fit them correctly. Their bodies stuttered. Their hitting hands were in better condition. Frightening him, they brutally and ruthlessly threw their fists at his nose and stopped in front of it. When he had recovered a little bit from the shock, they scared him again—they repeated that until he fell to his knees in front of them (!) trembling and tortured. When they stopped hurting him for pleasure, he very thankfully licked their shanks.

His secret longing for liberating Death—with long eyelashes that directed a serious and respectable gaze at him—was the misery of the oppressed. Sadly scratched open, he saw will-o'-the-wisps in the distance; he believed that death was flashing a promising signal at him.

For one more moment it seemed to him as if a new birth were beckoning, one whose severe pains he himself had to experience during the second entry into life.—In the closest *embryonic confinement* he sought for an open door into life—even if it was bedded between urine and excrement, between hair and flesh. He swore to himself, in the second life, if there were such a thing for him, he would suffer more *than was prescribed.*

His strength was at the point of giving out; only his spirit was still slightly alive.

Now the executioners stalked toward him, claiming their rights. On his own power and with a trembling body, he slowly straightened up against the pole. The weaker of the two held him by the shoulder. The stronger went to work on his head. He freed the neck from hair and thoroughly treated the head area. With a professional eye he looked up and down, winked at the man who was holding, then closed his fixed eyes.

He placed his hands around the throat, his thumbs on the Adam's apple, pressed with all his strength . . .

He broke his neck . . . but by then the judge was already dead. (F., the *coincidental stranger*, had judged himself.)

The neck-breaker turned apathetically away.

"Dignity as humanity's final stopping place needs no heroes," had been F.'s last thought.

After the killer had turned away without emotion, the broken-necked body of the condemned man crashed in a jumble to the ground:

One hand fell away from the rest of the body into the dirt. It was a slender-boned, white hand. At the top of the hand, light little hairs glittered and moved loosely in the evening wind. The hairline continued weakly up to the last segments of all the fingers—excluding the two thumbs. Then the keratin of the fingernails suddenly began. The entire surface of the nail appeared almost elliptical; for some surfaces the egg-shape was different and formed a distorted and not quite regular triangle. The two little fingers and the ring fingers had the longest nails. In the nail bed the keratin glowed pale red; as soon as it protruded over the tips of the fingers, the color ocher appeared. If these nails were dirty, he scraped off the dirt with a nail file that he often misused for other undertakings; it came off in the tiniest flecks and fell onto the tip of the finger flesh faster than he could think—from there he blew it away in a swirl.

The remaining horny finger coverings were cut as short as possible and ate their way into the nail bed to the point that it almost hurt. The nails of the forefingers and thumbs did not grow out flat but dug their growth directly into the flesh. He always had to cut these nails very short—that was hard work; the keratin was no thin sheet, it was hard and thick in structure, so that sweat-generating work was necessary while cutting or during the shortening process. After the cutting, blood trickled from the flesh of the nail bed. There was stinging pain.

They were sick nails that he had always wanted to have treated. Now it had become irrevocably unnecessary. He, in his entirety, was treated. Thoroughly.

Late at night the homicidal killers went away from the place of execution into the darkness—with them the fear that somebody could believe that in this case it was only a matter of a counterfeit suicide.

The two court-appointed professional murderers had turned up their collars, and the one with the hat wore it with the brim turned down deep over his face.

They were visibly agitated and groundlessly afraid of breaking the stillness of the night.

On the way to their storerooms they were accompanied by a queasy feeling in the region of their stomachs.

In doubt *regarding* the accused.

With the question: "Will they pardon the authorities for this *small* mistake?" on his lips, he died as though it were no death that strangled his life.

The victims of the court who are smeared by the law always yield themselves to the infernal enjoyment of revenge and the repulsive pleasure in the shedding of innocent blood.

And all of that is thoroughly indifferently written just in passing on their tortured bodies.

From their chests streams of blood unmanageably pour out at their feet—or their breath gives out. No matter what form of death, you hear only a few gurgling noises, sometimes death screams.

You must swallow your revulsion: *The external health of the laws hides decay and rottenness.*

Will they forgive the authorities for this *small* mistake?

Justitia has grown very old.

Those who wrote are now silent. Those who spoke now scream. Those who struck now murder.

Written in the late fall and winter of 1978, in Unterburg 5, on Lake Klopein.

AFTERWORD

The opening lines of *The Condemned Judge*, with their description of a statue of the blindfolded Justitia who has grown old, decrepit, and ugly as a result of neglect, rejection, and abandonment, present a stark and abrasive symbol for a modern society that has lost its sense of justice. In conveying his perceptions of an era that has relegated Justitia to a dark, dirty corner of the court cellar, Janko Ferk processes impulses from several facets of European cultural and political experience and tradition, including such diverse elements as the writings of Franz Kafka, the biblical portrayal of Christ, and the Nazi persecution of the Jews.

Although Ferk's literary concerns differ somewhat from those of Kafka, in many respects the framing image of the filthy, decaying statue introduces the reader to a new and even more oppressive and disturbing vision of the world of Kafka's novel *The Trial*, viewed through a lens that magnifies its degenerate nature, situations of alienation, and loss of humaneness. Unlike its predecessor, Ferk's narrative presents its material primarily from the point of view of agents of the court, rather than that of the defendant. Other elements, however, suggest that Kafka's work may have influenced Ferk directly in the creation of character relationships and specific scenes, as well as the exposition of the novel's central problem. *The Trial* and *The Condemned Judge* exhibit pertinent similarities in their respective depictions of the physical milieu, descriptions of interactions between court officers and those who must deal with them, treatments of the idea that all people are guilty, and portrayals of the final results of court action.

The primary setting for *The Condemned Judge* is a "Palace of the Law" located in an obscure side street. Like the precincts of the court in *The Trial*, the inside of the building is old and rundown; the temperature is oppressively warm; offices of court officials are located in remote corners of the attic. It is a place to which petitioners are drawn, and where they seem to spend their lives, unable to escape its compelling attraction while their cases move forward at an infinitely slow pace. And like Kafka's decaying bureaucratic legal machinery, Ferk's court appears to work continuously, around the clock. When his central characters leave their office for the day, their counterparts from the night shift are waiting impatiently in the corridor to take their places.

Ferk's portrayals of characteristic interactions between court officers and the people involved in legal cases are especially reminiscent of relationships in *The Trial*. Like Kafka's judges, Ferk's officials are inaccessible, and the petitioners desperately approach even the least significant employees of the court—from the janitors to the lowliest clerks—in the vain hope that such individuals have enough influence to help them. Nor do they have any more success than Kafka's characters. The defendants in pending trials are treated shabbily, abused, denied contact with higher authorities, and deprived of any information that might help them. As a result, they wait endlessly for the court's action and never really understand what is happening to them until they are convicted and sentenced to death.

In both novels the court proceeds on the assumption that all of the accused are guilty, and that acquittal will therefore be rare. However, the respective discussions of possible court action differ in at least two ways. Where Kafka describes the various potential outcomes in an "unofficial" conversation between his protagonist and a figure who is not a formal part of the legal machinery, Ferk incorporates his analysis of the verdict alternatives into an official document, the prosecuting attorney's statement. Moreover, while the major argument against acquittal in Kafka's court seems to be the actual predominance of guilt, Ferk's prosecutor defends the peculiar notion that regardless of guilt, acquittal is meaningless and therefore in the best interest of neither the defendant nor the society. Viewed in that light, *The Condemned Judge* presents a realm of existence that is subtly more horrifying than the world of Kafka's novel.

The most striking similarities between the two works are visible in the respective portrayals of how the sentences of the courts are carried out. In both accounts the figures who die accept their fates passively. Each is escorted to his place of execution by a shabby pair of executioners who hold their victim tightly between them, almost carrying him to his destiny. The executions occur at night and are accompanied by only trivial conversation. The executioners take off the victim's clothes, strike him, and grab him by the throat. Although Kafka's protagonist is then stabbed to death, while Ferk's judge dies of a broken neck, each of the descriptions directly suggests that some kind of mistake has been made and leaves the reader with the impression that something shameful has taken place.

In *The Condemned Judge*, the outrageous nature of the court's action is further emphasized in material that relates the situations of the condemned man, A., and the judge, Peter F., to scenes from the life (and death) of Christ. In his final confession, for example, A. identifies himself with Christ when he describes his birth in a barn and how he was wrapped in swaddling clothes. And although he is not crucified, he is hanged while wearing only a loincloth, and his executioners fight over his clothing in Ferk's version of two powerful images from the traditional account of the crucifixion.

The description of the judge's execution is even more pointed and direct in that regard. Not only do the court's mercenary killers argue over the judge's clothing, they also gamble for it in an obvious allusion to the Roman soldiers who cast lots for Christ's cloak at the foot of the cross.

There is a two-part message in Ferk's deliberate association of both the defendant A. and the judge with the figure of Christ. The execution of A. illustrates the point that by carrying out the death sentence the court commits a crime against all of humanity when it destroys someone who does not deserve to die. Peter F.'s fate, on the other hand, suggests that man may be subject to divine justice after all. In effect, his punishment is a graphic validation of Christ's famous admonition: "Judge not that ye be not judged" (Matthew 7:1).

From Ferk's perspective Christ is the perfect symbol for the innocent victim of a corrupt and inhumane system. But in order to make his point even more forcefully, the author also employs allusions to experience with which the German reader may more immediately identify. Visible illustrations of this point are found in formulations that compel the reader to make associations between elements of the novel and the historical world of Nazi Germany. To cite but one example: The judge is portrayed as sending the condemned men to their deaths with the words: *"TOD MACHT FREI"* (DEATH LIBERATES), in an obvious parody of the concentration-camp motto: *"Arbeit macht frei"* (work liberates). References to other Nazi slogans also occur, as do allusions to such political devices as the dictatorial decrees that gave the Nazi regime the authority to detain, confine, and kill politically undesirable people at will.

It would be easy to say that *The Condemned Judge* is simply a new version of Kafka's *The Trial* with some provocative twists that relate it more directly to general mortal experience, or, on a different level, to argue that the novel is primarily a strong indictment of capital punishment, and that it relies on a variety of devices that connect it to literary, historical, and cultural models, in order to make its message more compelling. Such interpretations, however, are fragmentary at best, because they fall short of probing the real depth of a novel that is both an important statement about the degeneration and death of positive, constructive human relationships in modern society, and a powerful admonition to turn the course of mankind's development in a more humane, compassionate, unselfish direction.

Lowell A. Bangerter, March 1992

ARIADNE PRESS

Translation Series:

February Shadows
By Elisabeth Reichart
Translated by Donna L. Hoffmeister
Afterword by Christa Wolf

Night Over Vienna
By Lili Körber
Translated by Viktoria Hertling
and Kay M. Stone. Commentary
by Viktoria Hertling

The Cool Million
By Erich Wolfgang Skwara
Translated by Harvey I. Dunkle
Preface by Martin Walser
Afterword by Richard Exner

Buried in the Sands of Time
Poetry by Janko Ferk
English/German/Slovenian
English Translation
by Herbert Kuhner

Puntigam or The Art of Forgetting
By Gerald Szyszkowitz
Translated by Adrian Del Caro
Preface by Simon Wiesenthal
Afterword by Jürgen Koppensteiner

Negatives of My Father
By Peter Henisch
Translated and with an Afterword
by Anne C. Ulmer

On the Other Side
By Gerald Szyszkowitz
Translated by Todd C. Hanlin
Afterword by Jürgen Koppensteiner

I Want to Speak
The Tragedy and Banality
of Survival in
Terezin and Auschwitz
By Margareta Glas-Larsson
Edited and with a Commentary
by Gerhard Botz
Translated by Lowell A. Bangerter

The Works of Solitude
By György Sebestyén
Translated and with an
Afterword by
Michael Mitchell

Remembering Gardens
By Kurt Klinger
Translated by Harvey I. Dunkle

Deserter
By Anton Fuchs
Translated and with an Afterword
by Todd C. Hanlin

From Here to There
By Peter Rosei
Translated and with an Afterword
by Kathleen Thorpe

The Angel of the West Window
By Gustav Meyrink
Translated by Michael Mitchell

Relationships
An Anthology of Contemporary
Austrian Literature
Selected and with an Introduction
by Adolf Opel

ARIADNE PRESS

Studies in Austrian Literature, Culture and Thought

*Major Figures of
Modern Austrian Literature*
Edited by
Donald G. Daviau

*Major Figures of
Turn-of-the-Century
Austrian Literature*
Edited by Donald G. Daviau

*Austrian Writers and the
Anschluss: Understanding the
Past—Overcoming the Past*
Edited by Donald G. Daviau

*Introducing Austria
A Short History*
By Lonnie Johnson

*Coexistent Contradictions
Joseph Roth in Retrospect*
Edited by
Helen Chambers

*The Verbal and Visual Art of
Alfred Kubin*
By Phillip H. Rhein

*Kafka and Language
In the Stream of
Thoughts and Life*
By G. von Natzmer Cooper

*Robert Musil and the Tradition
of the German Novelle*
By Kathleen O'Connor

*Austria in the Thirties
Culture and Politics*
Edited by Kenneth Segar
and John Warren

*Stefan Zweig:
An International Bibliography*
By Randolph J. Klawiter

*Austrian Foreign Policy
Yearbook*
Report of the Austrian Federal
Ministry for Foreign Affairs
for the Year 1990

*Quietude and Quest
Protagonists and Antagonists in
the Theater, on and off Stage
As Seen Through the Eyes of
Leon Askin*
Leon Askin and C. Melvin Davidson

*"What People Call Pessimism":
Sigmund Freud, Arthur Schnitzler
and Nineteenth-Century
Controversy at the University
of Vienna Medical School*
By Mark Luprecht

Arthur Schnitzler and Politics
By Adrian Clive Roberts

*Structures of Disintegration
Narrative Strategies in
Elias Canetti's* Die Blendung
By David Darby